THE GUNSMITH

476

Deadly Delivery

THE GUNSMITH

476

Deadly Delivery

J. R. Roberts

SPEAKING VOLUMES, LLC
NAPLES, FLORIDA
2022

Deadly Delivery

ISBN 978-1-64540-717-1

Chapter One

Davey Wilson was six years old when his parents died.

Well, they didn't just die, they were killed.

The day started like any other. His mother woke him for breakfast. His father had already been up and working for two hours. When Papa came in for breakfast, he washed up before sitting at the table and rubbing Davey's head.

"How's my boy?" his voice boomed loudly. His Papa's voice was always very loud.

"I'm good, Papa," Davey shouted, trying to match his father's timber.

"Davey," his mother chided him, "don't yell."

"Sorry, Mama."

"Why this boy has to yell, I don't know," Clay Wilson said.

"You don't?" his wife, Gloria, asked. "Don't you ever hear yourself? You yell everythin'! He's tryin' to be like his daddy."

"I don't yell," Clay said around a mouthful of flapjacks. "Maybe I talk loud, but I don't yell."

Gloria looked at Davey and said, "Papa yells, don't he?"

"Yeah!" Davey shouted. "Papa yells!" And he laughed and laughed . . .

***

After breakfast Clay took Davey out with him to plant what would be next year's crop of vegetables. Later in the afternoon, while they were working, some men rode onto the property.

Clay stopped and looked out at the three mounted riders who were approaching.

"Davey," Clay said, "go on inside the house."

"But Papa—"

"Do like I say, boy!" Clay snapped. "Inside. Tell Mama to take you down to the root cellar, and you both stay there until I come and getcha, you hear?"

"I hear, Papa."

Davey turned and ran to the house, but when he told his mother what his father had said, she didn't do it. She put him in the root cellar but didn't go down with him.

"You stay there until we come and get you, you hear me, Davey?"

"I hear ya, Mama, but Papa said—"

"You must do like I tell ya!" she yelled.

"Yes, Mama," Davey said, meekly.

His mother touched his face and said, "Mama loves you." And she closed the door-in-the-floor then covered it with a rug.

***

Davey heard the ruckus.

He heard his father shouting, heard other men yelling. Later, he heard footsteps in the house, more shouting, and then his mother screaming while men laughed.

Then it got quiet, until he heard the shots. After that he heard more footsteps all through the house. Finally, the men seemed to leave.

Davey waited a long time—hours that seemed like days to him. When he smelled smoke, he pushed with all his might to open the door. The first thing he saw when he climbed out was the fire and then his mother's body. She was partially naked, lying on her back, bleeding from between her breasts and her legs. The inside of the house was a shambles.

"Mama?" he said, standing over her. Flames were getting higher and hotter. The house was filling with smoke. He grabbed her hand and tried to pull her up, but he wasn't strong enough. Finally, the heat from the flame drove him outside.

3

When he stepped out, he didn't have far to go. His father's body was lying just at the top of the three steps in front of the door.

"Papa?"

He went to his father, saw the blood on his chest, reached down to take his hand and tug at him. The fire was taking the entire house now, including the wooden porch.

"Papa?"

But it soon became clear to him that his father was dead, like he now knew his mother was. He looked around, didn't see anyone else. There were no horses in the corral, the gate was wide open as was the barn door.

Davey didn't know what to do. He pulled and tugged at his father, but in the end, he was only able to tumble the body down the three steps and off the porch. There was nothing he could do to save his mother's body from burning, but maybe he had saved his father's. He sat down next to the body, tears streaming down his face. He didn't know how long he was there. When dusk came, he knew it would be dark soon, and he was afraid of the dark. He would have gone into the barn, but it was ablaze as well.

He laid next to his father's body and held his hand.

Chapter Two

Clint heard the shots, then saw the smoke.

Dusk was falling when he came within sight of the flames. It appeared a house and a barn were burning. He rode down to see if anybody needed help.

When he reached the two buildings, he immediately saw the small figure on the ground by a man's body. It was a small boy.

The boy looked up at him, his dirty face stained with tear tracks. Clint knew the smudges weren't from dirt, but smoke. The boy had been in the fire.

"Is that your father?" Clint asked.

"Yes, Sir."

Clint stared down at the body, saw the bullet holes.

"Where's your mother?"

"She was inside," the boy said. "I couldn't get her out, Mister. I tried."

"How'd you get your father out?"

"He was outside, Mister. I could only roll him down the steps."

"I heard shots," Clint said. "Who shot him?"

"I dunno," the boy said. "I was in the root cellar. They told me not to come out. But I heard some men laughing, and my mother screaming, and then . . . and then I saw the smoke, so I come out."

"And found your parents."

The boy nodded.

"What's your name, son?"

"Davey," the boy said, "Davey Wilson."

"How old are you?"

"Five."

This was a hell of a thing for a five-year-old boy to see.

"You can't stay here, Davey," Clint said. "You'll have to come with me."

"W-where?"

"What's the nearest town?"

"Kellog," Davey said. "My Ma and Pa go there for supplies, sometimes to eat in the hotel."

"Is there a sheriff there?"

"Yeah," Davey said. "Sheriff Caldwell."

"Okay," Clint said, reaching down, "let's go."

"What about my Ma and Pa, Mister?"

"We'll have to wait until the fire dies down to get your mother out," Clint said. "The sheriff will send somebody to bring them into town to the undertaker. Then they'll be buried."

The boy stood up, reached for Clint's hand so he could be hauled up into the saddle in front of the man.

"Is there anybody in town you can stay with?"

"Sometimes Mrs. Hinton looks out for me."

"Okay," Clint said. "We'll go see the sheriff, and then take you to Mrs. Hinton."

"O-okay, Mister."

"My name's Clint, Davey. Call me Clint."

"O-okay, Clint."

The boy lowered his head and cried as Clint rode them away from the scene.

***

It was dark by the time they rode into Kellog. It was dark enough for some of the townspeople to have seen the glow of the fire in the distance. Some of them had gathered in front of a saloon. Clint heard them wondering where the fire was. They paid little interest to him and the boy riding in.

Clint kept riding until he saw the sheriff's office. He reined in his Tobiano in front of it, dismounted and lifted Davey off the saddle.

"Let's talk to the sheriff, Davey," he said, and carried the boy to the door.

When Clint entered the office, the man behind the desk got to his feet and immediately came around.

"Who Are you?" he demanded. "What are you doin' with this boy?"

"My name's Clint Adams, Sheriff," Clint said. "I found this boy outside his burning house. Both of his parents are dead."

"Dead?" the sheriff said. "The Wilsons? That's their place that's burnin'?"

"That's it. The father was shot, the mother was in the house. I assume she burned to death or was already dead when the fire started."

"Are you okay, Davey?"

"No, Sir, I'm not," Davey said, sniffling. "They killed my Ma and Pa."

"Who did?"

"Some men."

"Did you see them?"

"No, Sir," he said, "but I heard 'em."

"Are you Sheriff Caldwell?"

"I am," the man said. He was tall, rangy, in his late thirties.

"You'll have to send someone out there to collect the Wilsons," Clint said. "She was in the house, he's lying outside."

"I'll get some men and go out there right now," Caldwell said. "Will you come along?"

"Davey told me about someone named Mrs. Hinton," Clint said. "He says she takes care of him, sometimes. Do you know who she is?"

"Yeah, Madeleine Hinton. She lives in a big house at the north end of town."

"Then I'll take the boy over there and meet you out there," Clint said.

"That suits me," Caldwell said. "I'll talk to the boy some more in the mornin', after he's had some sleep and I've had a look."

"And that suits me," Clint said. He looked at the boy in his arms. "Come on, Davey."

"Sheriff?"

"Yeah, Davey?"

"Are you gonna catch the men who killed my Ma and Pa?" the boy asked.

"I'm sure gonna try, Davey."

Clint, still carrying the boy, turned and left. They mounted the Tobiano and rode to the north end of town to find Mrs. Hinton's house.

Chapter Three

"That's it!" Davey cried, pointing to an impressive two-story house.

Clint reined in, tied the horse and once again carried the boy, who by this time was exhausted, to the door. He knocked and waited. The door was opened by an attractive, middle-aged woman with long dark hair and blue eyes. When she saw the boy, she reacted immediately.

"Davey! Are you all right? What's happened?"

"They killed Ma and Pa, Aunt Maddy," Davey said.

"What?" She looked at Clint. "Is that true?"

"I'm afraid it is, Ma'am."

"And who are you?" she asked. "Why do you have Davey?"

"This is Mister Clint, Aunt Maddy," the boy said. "He saved me."

"Saved him?"

"Actually," Clint said, "I found him sitting on the ground outside the burning house."

"Burning? My God!"

"Davey told me that you sometimes care for him," Clint said. "I have to ride back out to the house and meet the sheriff. I was hoping you'd take him."

"Of course," she said, opening her arms. "Come here, you poor darling."

Clint handed the boy over to her.

"Oh yes," she said, wrinkling her nose, "you smell of smoke. I'm going to give you a nice warm bath and then put you to bed."

"A bath?" the boy said, alarmed.

She looked at Clint.

"You do what you have to do, Mister—"

"Adams, Ma'am," he said. "Clint Adams."

"I assume the sheriff will be by to talk with Davey tomorrow."

"Yes, Ma'am."

"Will you come and see me, Mr. Clint?" Davey asked.

"I'll be back, Davey," Clint said. "Don't you worry."

"Then we'll see you in the morning, Mr. Adams," Maddy Hinton said, and closed the door."

Clint mounted his Tobiano and headed out to the Wilson house.

***

When he reached the house, the fires were both raging and none of the half dozen men there were making any attempts to put them out.

While the sheriff gave directions, the men moved the body of Mr. Wilson onto the back of a buckboard. As Clint dismounted, he heard the sheriff shouting.

"We'll have to wait for the fire to die down before we can recover Mrs. Wilson's body."

"Can't we come back later, Sheriff?" one man asked. "My wife's got supper waitin'."

"These structures are gonna collapse any minute," the sheriff said. "The fire should die down soon after that. We're gonna wait."

He turned to watch Clint walk towards him.

"We found Wilson at the base of the steps," he said.

"Davey said he rolled his father down to get him away from the fire. He said he tried to move his mother but couldn't."

"That's quite a boy," Caldwell said.

"Yes, he is," Clint said.

"We'll have to wait til daylight to see if we can pick up any tracks," Caldwell said. "Unfortunately, I'm pretty sure we trampled most of them, already."

"There still might be some out there," Clint said, waving. "You might at least find out which way they lit out."

The sheriff turned and looked at the burning house, which was now partially collapsed.

"You know," Clint said, "you could send these men back to town with the body. You and I can wait here til daylight."

"Yeah, you're probably right," the lawman said. "They could come back with the buckboard, later. I'll let 'em, know."

While the sheriff went to talk to his men, Clint turned and watched the fire. He wondered if Davey was going to be helpful at all in finding out who was responsible for this.

Chapter Four

After the other men had headed back to town with Wilson's body, the sheriff produced a whiskey bottle and passed it to Clint as they watched the fire.

"What brings the Gunsmith to Kellog?" the lawman asked.

"Davey," Clint said, taking a swig and handing the bottle back. "I was just looking for a place to camp when I heard the shots and saw the fire."

"You heard the shots?" Caldwell said. "You didn't see anythin'?"

"No," Clint said. "By the time I got there, whoever had killed the Wilsons were gone."

"What did Davey say he saw?" the sheriff asked.

"Nothing," Clint said. "He was in the root cellar. But he heard a lot. I think he heard his mother being raped and murdered."

"Jesus!" Caldwell swore. "That poor kid. They were nice people, you know? And he's a good kid."

"Well, I didn't question him very much," Clint said. "When you talk to him tomorrow maybe you can get something else out of him."

"Like what?" Caldwell asked. "If he was hidin' in the root cellar . . ." The man shrugged.

"Well," Clint said, "maybe he heard something helpful."

That made Caldwell brighten up.

"Like maybe a name!" he said.

Or maybe one of them had a voice he'd remember," Clint offered.

"I wonder why they didn't look in the root cellar," Caldwell said.

"Could be none of them grew up on a farm," Clint said. "They just didn't think of it."

"Well," Caldwell said, "if they're from around here, we better not let it be known that the boy heard anythin'."

"That's a good thought," Clint agreed. "If they're not from around here, will you be gettin' a posse together?"

"I probably will," the lawman said. "And I'd appreciate it if you'd come along."

"Like I said," Clint told him, "I never even heard of Kellog when I was riding by."

"Were you goin' someplace special?"

"Not really . . ."

"Then maybe you can stay and help out."

Clint reclaimed the whiskey bottle from the man.

"Maybe," he said. "We'll see."

***

By the time a few of the men returned at daylight with the buckboard, the house and barn were just smoldering rubble.

"We got the body to the undertakers, sheriff," one of the men said.

"Thanks, Milo. We ought to be able to get in there and find Mrs. Wilson's body soon."

"There probably ain't much left of it," Milo said.

"Maybe not, but we owe her a decent burial."

They waited a while longer until they could wade through the rubble without danger of being burned. Most of what they trod over simply crumbled beneath their weight.

"There she is," Caldwell said.

There were some bones left, bleached white by the heat.

"Let's wrap these in a blanket and take them to the undertaker," Caldwell said.

They stowed the wrapped bones on the back of the buckboard.

"Take 'em to town, Milo."

"What about you?"

"Me and Adams are gonna see if we can pick up a trail," the lawman said, "We'll see you in town later."

"Right."

He and the other men headed for town with the buck-board. Clint and Caldwell mounted their horses.

"I ain't much of a tracker," the sheriff admitted.

"I'm no expert, but I've done my fair share," Clint said. "Let me see what I can find."

As the sheriff had mentioned, in the dark he and his men had trampled over most of the tracks left by the killers. Clint chose to ride further away from the house in search of a fairly fresh sign.

"Anythin'?" the sheriff asked.

"We're pretty far from the house," Clint said. "There are some tracks, but the question is, whose?"

"How many?"

"I see three."

"Headin' which way?"

"Back to town."

Caldwell thought about that, then said, "Could be any-body's tracks."

"That's right," Clint said. "Let's make a circle around the house and see if I find any more."

"Sure."

The fact that the tracks were heading to town seemed to bother the lawman. If it was possible that the Wilsons had been killed by somebody from town, then it was probably somebody he knew.

Chapter Five

There were no more tracks around the house.

"Nobody really rides out here," Caldwell said. "The Wilsons come to town a couple of times a month for supplies."

"What about friends?" Clint asked. "Who were their friends?"

"No one that I know of," Caldwell said, "except for Maddy Hinton."

"What's the story with her?"

"She was friends with Gloria Wilson."

"Not with the father?"

"Not that I know of," Caldwell said. "Just Gloria. And she loved Davey and took care of him when they came to town to shop."

"I guess we better get back," Clint said. "We've got to keep news from getting around that Davey survived the fire. We don't need to have those killers gunning for him."

"Good point," Caldwell said.

They turned their horses and rode hard to get back to town.

***

When they got back to town, they immediately went to Maddy Hinton's house. Clint knocked on the door, impatiently. It was finally answered by Mrs. Hinton, who was tying her robe around her waist.

"Oh, it's you gentlemen," she said. "I hope you don't want me to wake poor Davey."

"No," Caldwell said, "we just wanted to make sure you haven't talked with anyone about him."

"Why would I?" she asked.

"Somebody might have asked," the lawman said. "We don't want word gettin' out that he survived. The killers might decide to come back for him."

"Well, I'm not going to say anything," she assured him, "but what about your own men?"

"I'll be talkin' to them, next," he said.

She looked past the sheriff and asked Clint, "Would you like to come in, Mr. Adams?"

"Not at the moment, Mrs. Hinton," Clint said. "I'll be going with the sheriff as he talks to his men."

"Then why don't you return later and have breakfast with Davey?"

"I'll do that, Ma'am."

"And for Pete's sake, don't call me 'Ma'am.' "

She slammed the door.

***

They found each man individually and were assured by each of them that not a word had been said about the boy.

But the last man, Milo, added, "Of course, we did tell the undertaker."

"Goddamn it!" the sheriff swore.

He and Clint headed for the undertaker's office.

***

"Of course I haven't said a word, Sheriff," Wendell Zack said.

"That's good, Mr. Zack."

"Well," the elderly undertaker added, "except for Mr. Keller."

"Mike Keller?" Caldwell said. "Jesus!"

"Who's Mike Keller?" Clint asked.

"The editor of the local newspaper," Caldwell answered.

"Why would you tell him?" Clint demanded of the undertaker.

"Well," Zack said, "he asked."

"We better get to him before he goes to press," Caldwell said, and they left the bewildered looking undertaker.

***

When they got to the office of *The Kellog Sentinel*, they found the door locked. Caldwell banged his fist on it.

"Okay, okay!" a voice boomed from inside. A thick-set man in his thirties who looked more like a bartender than a newspaperman came to the door and opened it.

"Sheriff Caldwell," he said. "What can I do for you?"

"Let us in, Mike."

"Sure."

He backed away to allow Caldwell and Clint to enter and close the door behind them.

"What's this about, Sheriff?"

"The Wilson fire," Caldwell said.

"I heard about it."

"That's why we're here," Caldwell said. "Are you gonna write about it?"

Keller folded his arms across his burly chest.

"Whatayou think?" he asked. "It's a story. Whattay-ou think?"

"You can't write about the boy," Caldwell said.

"Davey Wilson survives the murder of his parents and the burnin' of his home?" Keller said. "You bet I wrote about it."

"Keller," Caldwell said, "you can't—"

"Wait a minute," Clint cut him off. "Wrote about it?"

"You bet," Keller said. "I came in early, wrote it, got it printed and out."

"It's already out there?" Caldwell asked.

Keller reached over, grabbed a newspaper and handed it to Caldwell, who held it so he and Clint could both read it.

FIVE YEAR OLD SURVIVES MURDER AND ARSON OF WILSON FAMILY.

"Jesus!" Clint said.

Chapter Six

"Did you even talk to the boy?" Caldwell asked.

"No," Keller said. "Why would I? I'm not a monster. He's probably in shock. I'll wait til he sees the doctor."

"If he gets a chance to see a doctor," Clint said.

"And why wouldn't he?" Keller asked.

"Because you just told the killers that they missed the boy," Clint said. "They won't know whether or not he can identify them."

"So they'll just kill 'im," Caldwell said.

"Wow," Keller said, "what a story. Child can identify killers of his parents."

"You can't print that!" the lawman said.

"Why not?" Keller asked. "It's up to you to protect him. That's your job. Writin' about this is mine."

"Are you crazy?" Clint asked.

"Who's this guy?" Keller asked, pointing.

"This is Clint Adams. He found the boy sittin' next to his father's body."

"The Gunsmith found the boy?" Keller asked, excitedly. "What a story!"

"If you write about me," Clint said, "you won't be happy with the consequences."

"Are you threatenin' me?"

"I'm just warning you," Clint said. "Don't write about me without my permission."

Keller looked at the sheriff.

"He's threatenin' the press, Sheriff."

"So am I!" Caldwell said. "Don't write a word more about this until you hear from me."

"Is that some sort of order, Sheriff?"

"Like you said, Mike," Caldwell answered. "It's a threat."

Caldwell and Clint left the office.

"He was right about one thing," Clint said.

"What was that?"

"That boy needs to be seen by a doctor."

"I'll have Doc Pegram go to Mrs. Hinton's house," the sheriff said.

"I'll get over there now and have breakfast with the boy," Clint said. "Maybe he'll remember something."

"I'll see you there later," the lawman said, and they split up.

***

Clint went directly to Maddy Hinton's house.

"I'm happy to see you," she said, at the door. "Davey's ready for his breakfast."

She was still wearing her robe, but he noticed she had combed her hair and applied some make-up to her lovely face.

She led him through a lushly lined living room to the kitchen, where Davey was sitting at the table. He was wearing a pair of green pajamas.

"Clint! You're here!"

"Hiya, Davey," Clint said. "Those are great pajamas."

"I wear 'em whenever I stay here," the boy said. "Aunt Maddy bought 'em for me."

"Have a seat," Maddy Hinton told him. "Ham-and-eggs okay?"

"That's fine," Clint said.

"It's my favorite!" Davey said.

Maddy laid their plates on the table, then gave Clint a cup of coffee and Davey a glass of milk. She then seated herself with a plate and coffee.

"What happened out there?" she asked.

Clint looked at Davey.

"It's all right," she said. "Davey told me as much as he knows."

"Or remembers," Clint said. "Maybe he can remember more."

"I don't mind if he hears us talk," she said, "but I don't want you to question him."

"The sheriff's going to bring Doc Pegram here to check him out."

"Good."

"The doctor!" Davey said, alarmed.

"Just to look you over, champ," Clint said. "To make sure the fire and smoke didn't hurt you."

"It didn't hurt me," Davey insisted.

Maddy reached her hand out and laid it on Davey's arm.

"He's just going to make sure, darling." She rubbed his arm. "Eat your breakfast."

She looked at Clint.

"I'm eating mine," he said.

"So, what happened out there?"

"We recovered what we could, and brought it back," he said. "They can be . . . interred tomorrow."

"What's 'terred?" Davey asked.

"We're going to bury your parents, Davey," she said, "so they can be with God."

"In Heaven?"

"That's right," she said. "In Heaven."

The boy continued to eat. Clint sent a questioning look Maddy's way, but she shook him off.

She asked Clint where he was going and what he was doing when he found Davey. He told her he was drifting, looking for a place to camp.

"What's driftin'?" Davey asked.

Clint explained that riding to just ride, with nowhere to go, was drifting.

When Davey finished his breakfast Maddy said, "Why don't you go and wait in your room until the doctor comes?"

"Doctor," Davey said, with distaste. "Will you be here when he comes?" he asked Clint.

"I'll be here."

Davey ran from the kitchen to go and play in his room.

"He doesn't seem to be very upset about losing his parents," Clint said.

"I think he's in a state of shock, Mr. Adams," she said. "But we'll know more when the doctor gets here. More coffee?"

Chapter Seven

"You said you found as much as you could," Maddy said. "What did that mean?"

"We found some of Mrs. Wilson's bones," Clint said. "They'll be buried along with her husband's body."

"I don't think Davey should watch that," she said.

"I agree. The boy's seen enough."

"More coffee?" she asked.

"Please."

She cleared the breakfast plates away, then poured him another cup and sat across from him.

"I suppose the sheriff is going to look for the killers?" she asked.

"He is," Clint said. "What tracks we could find seemed to be leading back to town."

That shocked her.

"So they were killed by somebody from town?"

"That's the way it looks."

"Does anybody know about Davey? That he survived?"

For the first time, he told her about the newspaper editor.

"Keller!" she spat. "He doesn't care about anything but his paper. Those killers could come after Davey."

"That's the way the sheriff and I saw it, too," Clint said. "We can't leave him here. It would also put you in danger."

"Then where?" she asked. "And what about you? Are you going to stay around?"

"I can't leave while that boy's in danger," he said.

"I'm glad to hear you say that, Mr. Adams."

"Just call me, Clint, Miss Hinton."

"It's Mrs.," she said. "I'm a widow. But you can call me Maddy."

There was a knock at the front door at that point.

"Who's that?" she asked, starting to get up.

"Should be the sheriff, with the doctor," he said, waving her down. "I'll get it, just in case."

Clint left the kitchen and went to the front door. He looked out the window to confirm it was the law and the sawbones, then opened the door.

"Clint Adams," Sheriff Caldwell said, "meet Doc Pegram."

"Doctor," Clint said, shaking hands with the tall, fiftyish man.

"Where's the boy?" Pegram asked.

"He's in his room," Clint said.

From behind him Maddy said, "I'll take you back, Doc."

"And stay with us while I examine him, Maddy," the doctor said.

"Right."

She led him to the back of the house.

"Is that coffee I smell?" Caldwell asked.

"Come into the kitchen. There might even be a couple of slices of ham left."

The lawman followed Clint into the kitchen . . .

***

Frank Henderson rushed into the saloon, holding a copy of the town newspaper in his hand. He looked around, located Jimbo Collins and rushed over to him.

"Have you s-s-seen this?" he demanded, fighting his stammer.

"Seen what? Relax, Frank. Get yourself a beer."

"T-t-this!" Henderson said, pushing the newspaper into Jimbo's face.

Jimbo read the headline, then grabbed the paper from Henderson's hand.

"There was a kid?" he demanded. "I didn't see no kid."

"I d-d-didn't either, but this s-s-ays he was u-u-under the floor."

"Damn!" Jimbo said. "What'd he see and hear?"

"I d-d-dunno."

"Well," Jimbo said, "find Coyote. He's probably in the whorehouse. We gotta do somethin' about this."

"R-r-right."

As Henderson started to turn away, Jimbo said, "Hey."

"What?"

"Where's the kid now?"

"The newspaper don't s-s-say."

"Okay, okay," Jimbo said. "Go!"

Henderson ran out. The man's stammer usually drove Jimbo a little nuts, but at least he got the words out.

A kid! They never should've missed that.

***

Clint and Caldwell were drinking another cup of coffee when Maddy came into the kitchen with Doc Pegram.

"How's the boy, Doc?" Caldwell asked.

"Maddy was right," Pegram said. "He's in a mild state of shock. Nothing serious, but he's keeping his feelings inside."

"What happens when his feelings come out?" Clint asked.

"Who knows?" Pegram said. "Tears? Hysteria? We'll have to wait and see."

"Thanks, Doc," Caldwell said.

"Sure thing," Doc Pegram said.

"I'll see you to the door, doctor," Maddy said.

They left the room.

"What do we do with the boy?" Caldwell said. "I mean, to keep him safe."

"I don't know," Clint said. "We can't let him stay here. Maddy would be in danger, as well."

"I don't care about that," she said, coming back into the room. "But I have an idea."

"What?" Caldwell said.

"Davey has an uncle."

"He has a relative?" Clint asked. "Where?"

"San Francisco," she said.

"What does he do there?" Clint asked.

"I don't know," she said. "Gloria just told me her brother-in-law lived there."

"Do you know his name?" Clint asked.

"Yes."

"Address?"

"Not exactly," Maddy said, "but I understood from some of the things Gloria said about her brother-in-law that he could be found in or around Portsmouth Square.

"So he's a gambler," Clint said. "I should be able to find him."

"By going there?" she asked.

"I'll start with some telegrams," Clint said. "Meanwhile, I'll keep the boy with me."

"I have a better idea," she said. "Why don't you just move in here for the time being? I can care for Davey, and you can look after both of us."

"That doesn't sound bad," Sheriff Caldwell said. "Meanwhile, I'll see if I can find out who the killers are."

"I suppose that's the best way to go, for now," Clint agreed.

"Good," Maddy said, "I'll plan a lovely dinner for you and Davey. Would you like to join us, Sheriff?"

"That'd be nice," he said. "But don't plan on me. I'll make it if I can."

"I'll walk you out so I can get my things from my horse. Would you board him for me?"

"I'll take care of it, Clint."

"I'll be right back, Maddy," Clint said.

He and the lawman walked outside. The lawman waited while Clint grabbed his rifle, saddle bags and bedroll.

"I'll see you later, Adams."

"Good luck," Clint said, and went back into the house.

Chapter Eight

"This will be your room," Maddy told Clint. "Davey's just next door, and I'm down the hall."

"That's fine."

"I must tell you, I feel so much safer with you here, Clint."

"I hope Davey feels the same way," he said.

"You could probably use a bath after the day you've had," she said. "I can prepare it for you."

Clint knew he smelled of smoke from the fire, so he said, "That'd be great."

"I'll let you know when it's ready," she said, then left him alone.

He put his rifle and bedroll in a corner, set his saddlebags down on the bed. Normally, when in a hotel he would remove his gunbelt, but in the house he intended to keep it on.

He wondered, if the killers knew Clay and Gloria Wilson, what reason could they have had to kill them? But if they did know that couple, wouldn't they have known about Davey? No, they could have been sent to kill the adults by someone who didn't tell the killers about the boy.

"Your bath is ready," Maddy said, appearing at the door. "Nice and hot."

"Thank you."

"It's down at the far end of the hall," she said. "There are clean towels."

"Thanks, Maddy."

She left him to it.

***

Henderson found Coyote in the whorehouse.

The half breed liked being with white women— usually blondes.

He was in an upstairs room, pounding into a blonde from behind, holding her hips in his hands. She moaned and groaned loudly because she knew he liked hearing that. The more she reacted, the more he paid.

When there was a knock at the door he yelled, "Come on in!"

The door opened and Henderson stepped in. He wasn't surprised because he knew where he was, and what the half breed liked.

"Sorry to interrupt," he said.

"I am not stopping," Coyote said, "so go ahead and say what you came to say."

The blonde looked over at Henderson, gave him a smile, and then went back to moaning. Henderson couldn't take his eyes from her pendulous, swaying breasts.

"Jimbo wants us," Henderson said.

"Is there a problem?"

"Yeah, there is," Henderson said. "There may have been a witness we missed."

The blonde turned to look over her shoulder at Coyote, who slapped her on her big ass hard enough to leave a red mark.

"Keep your mind on your own business," he told her.

She nodded and began to lunge back at him in time to his pounding.

"This should not take much longer," he told Henderson.

"I'll wait downstairs."

Henderson backed out, taking one last look at the naked blonde, and then closed the door behind him.

A few more strokes and Coyote roared as he emptied himself into the blonde, then pushed her away.

"Same time tomorrow?" she asked, while he was getting dressed.

"If I am in town, yes," he said. "And have another girl here."

"Tina?" she asked. "The little blonde."

"Yes," he said. "She will be good."

He put money down on the dresser and left.

The blonde, Lisa, rubbed her ass where he had slapped her.

***

There was a timid knock at the door.

"Come in," Clint said.

When the door opened slowly, Clint started to reach for the gun he had placed next to the bathtub on a chair. But when Davey's head popped in, he relaxed.

"Hey, champ," he said. "Come on in."

"Aunt Maddy made you take a bath, too, huh?" Davey asked, stepping in.

"She sure did," Clint said.

Davey made a face.

"I hate baths," he said. "Do you?"

"Not me," Clint said. "I find a hot bath to be relaxing."

"Yuch!" Davey said.

Clint splashed some water the boy's way, making Davey jump back, and then they both laughed.

"Why don't you get out of here so I can finish," Clint said. "Or do you want me to drag you in here?"

"No! No!" the boy yelled, and ran out, laughing.

Clint climbed out of the tub, dried off, and got dressed, putting on his only clean shirt. He strapped on his gun and left the room.

He found Maddy sitting on the sofa with Davey, reading to the boy.

"Clint, Aunt Maddy's readin' me Tom Sawyer."

"By Mark Twain," Clint said. "He's a friend of mine."

"Really?" Davey asked.

"Really?" Maddy asked. "What's he like?"

"One of a kind," Clint said. "There's nobody like him."

"That's amazing," she said. "The gunman and the writer." Then she realized what she had said. "Oh, I'm sorry."

"Don't be," Clint said. "That's the reputation I have. There's nothing I can do about it."

"It's just an odd pairing, don't you think?" she asked.

"Definitely."

"I wanna do somethin' else," Davey announced.

"All right," Maddy said, closing the book. "What?"

"I wanna play cards," he said. "You know how to play cards, Clint?"

"I know a few card games, Davey," Clint answered. "What did you have in mind?"

"I wanna play poker."

That surprised Clint.

"You know how to play poker?" he asked.

"My pa taught me."

Clint looked at Maddy.

"Do you have any cards?"

***

"What took you so goddamn long?" Jimbo asked as Coyote and Henderson entered the saloon.

Henderson just looked over at Coyote.

"There are some things you cannot leave unfinished," the half breed said.

"Yeah, right," Jimbo said. "Siddown."

They sat.

"Frank, get some beers."

Henderson sighed heavily and got up. He went to the bar and came back with three beers.

"Did you show him?" Jimbo asked Henderson.

"N-n-no."

"Show me what?"

They put the newspaper in front of him. Coyote read the headline.

"So?"

"So that kid might be able to identify us," Jimbo said.

"Then kill him," Coyote said.

"Before we can kill 'im, we gotta find 'im," Jimbo said.

"Who do you think knows where he is?" Coyote asked.

"I'm pretty sure the sheriff would," Jimbo said, "but probably the newspaper editor."

"Then we should ask him," Coyote said.

"I think you and Frank should do just that," Jimbo said.

Chapter Nine

Maddy was about to put dinner on the table for the three of them—and a place for the sheriff if he appeared—when there was a knock on the door.

"I'll get it," Clint said.

He opened the door and found the sheriff standing there.

"Just in time for dinner," Clint said.

"Oh!" Caldwell said, "I wasn't even thinkin' about that."

"Well," Clint said. "Come on in. What brought you here?"

"I got news."

Clint turned and looked at the kitchen door.

"Is it something Davey shouldn't hear?"

"Maybe."

"Well, let's have it, then."

"Mike Keller's at the doc's," Caldwell said. "Somebody gave him a good beatin'."

"What for?"

"He hasn't regained consciousness yet, but I think we can guess."

"Looking for Davey?"

Caldwell nodded.

"That's my guess," he said.

"You think he told them?"

"Who knows?" Caldwell said. "Keller's a hard nose when it comes to his paper, but this is entirely different. I don't know how he'd react to somethin' like this."

"Well," Clint said, "if he took the beating, maybe he didn't talk."

"Maybe."

"There's another thing, though."

"What?"

"Does he even know where the boy is?"

Caldwell frowned.

"Probably not," he answered, "though he might've guessed."

"Let's not discuss this in front of Davey," Clint said. "I don't want to set him off. Come on, Maddy's putting the food on the table."

They entered the kitchen together.

"Ah, you made it, Sheriff," she said.

"I could smell it from my office," he told her.

"Liar! Take off your hat and sit."

He hung his hat on the back of the chair and seated himself across from Davey.

"Hi, Sheriff."

"Hey, Davey," the lawman said. "How are you doin'?"

"Me and Clint've been playin' poker," the boy said, happily.

"Is that right? Who's winnin'?"

"I am!" Davey announced, proudly.

"He's a natural," Clint said. "Draws to an inside straight and makes it."

Maddy came to the table with plates of pot roast.

"The boy shouldn't be gambling," she said.

"Aw, Aunt Maddy," Davey said. "It's fun."

She sat down and looked him in the eye.

"It's fun when you're winning, Davey," she said. "Not so much fun when you're losing."

"That's true, Davey," Clint said.

"But I'm winning," the boy insisted. "I always won when I played Pa."

"That might change, Davey," Clint said, looking at Maddy, who nodded. It was time to stop letting the boy win.

They tried to talk about anything but the Wilsons, finishing their meal. When they were done, Davey cried out, "More poker."

"You boys go ahead," Maddy said. "I'll clean up."

Clint, the lawman, and Davey stood and left the kitchen together.

Chapter Ten

For the next half hour Davey was losing his toothpicks. Clint had decided to play the boy for the sticks,
not money. As he lost, Davey became frustrated.

"Your takin' all my toothpicks," he complained.

"Your Aunt Maddy told you, it's not as much fun
when you're losin'," Sheriff Caldwell told him. The man
looked at Clint. "I'm gonna go to my office. I'll see you
in the mornin'. Good-night, Davey."

" 'night Sheriff."

Clint dealt and they looked at their cards while the
sheriff left. Maddy came into the room, sat and watched
for a while.

"You beat me again!" Davey complained.

"All right, Davey," Maddy said, rising, "time for
bed."

"But I still have some sticks!"

"You can lose them tomorrow."

He stood up and said, "I'm gonna win tomorrow."

As Davey ran ahead to his room, Clint grabbed Maddy's arm.

"See if he remembers his uncle's name."

"Right."

She followed the boy upstairs to his room. Clint sat on the sofa to wait, wishing he had a beer.

"Would you like a drink?" she asked, when she came back down.

"I'd like a beer, but I'll take whatever you've got."

"Whiskey."

"Fine."

She went to a cabinet, opened it, poured two drinks and brought them to the sofa. She handed one to Clint and sat with him.

"This is not the rot gut you'd get in a saloon," she said. "It's good Irish whiskey."

Clint sipped it, found it no different from any other whiskey he'd had. He still preferred beer.

"What'd you get from Davey?"

"All he knows is Uncle Billy," she said.

"If Gloria said it was her brother-in-law, then his name is Billy, or William, Wilson. If he's in Portsmouth Square, I should be able to find him."

"Will you go to look for him?"

"I have some contacts there," Clint replied. "I'll send a few telegrams. If we locate him, I'll see if he'll take the boy. If he says yes, I'll take Davey there."

"That'll take some time," she said. "You're willing to make that commitment?"

"The boy needs help," he said. "That's worth the commitment."

"You're quite a man to take that on," she commented.

"I didn't ask for the job," he said. "But I found the boy, and I can't just walk away."

"Yes," she said, moving closer, "quite a man."

***

"You killed him?" Jimbo demanded.

"We didn't kill 'im," Henderson said. "We gave him a beatin'."

"How bad?"

"He was taken to the doctor," Coyote said.

"But he's alive?"

"He was when we left," Henderson said.

Jimbo looked around the saloon to be sure no one was listening to their conversation.

"Why was it necessary to beat him that bad?" Jimbo asked.

"He wouldn't talk," Henderson said.

"He said he didn't know where the boy was," Coyote said.

"Maybe he was tellin' the truth," Jimbo said.

"We just wanted to be sure," Henderson said. "We didn't know he'd pass out like that. He seemed to be pretty strong."

"He's a newspaperman," Jimbo said. "Their strength is on paper."

"What do we do now?" Coyote said.

"Ask around town," Jimbo said. "Just make it sound like you're curious. Somebody may have seen when they brought the boy in."

"Okay," Henderson said. "We can do that tomorrow."

"Start tonight," Jimbo said, "in the saloons. They've gotta be talkin' about the fire and the bodies. Split up, you'll cover more ground that way."

"The saloons," Henderson said.

"And the whorehouse," Coyote said.

Jimbo looked at him.

"You never know what those girls might hear," Coyote explained.

"Yeah, okay," Jimbo said. "Just get to it."

As both men stood up and left the saloon, Jimbo knew what Coyote was planning to do in the whorehouse, but he might actually get those girls to talking.

Jimbo sat back and tried to pick up some of the conversations going on around him. Maybe he'd be lucky enough to pick something up. He waved to one of the saloon girls for another beer.

***

Maddy came close enough to Clint to press her hip to his. He could feel the heat of her body. They both drank some more, and then their mouths came together in a whiskey-soaked kiss.

"We should adjourn to my bedroom, just in case Davey comes down."

"Lead the way," he told her.

She rose, took his hand and led him up the stairs and to her bedroom. Once there she closed the door, and they pressed their bodies together in another hot kiss.

Clint had been wondering how to spend his time once his poker partner went to bed. This seemed as good—or better—as anything.

They broke their kiss and he helped her divest herself of her clothing. In turn, she helped him unstrap his gunbelt, which he hung on her bedpost. That done, they both removed his clothes, starting with his boots.

When that was done, they stood back and looked at each other.

Chapter Eleven

Locked in a hot embrace, burning flesh to burning flesh, Clint and Maddy tumbled onto the bed together. Clint enjoyed the cushiony feel of her curves. Maddy was over forty, but all that did was sweeten her flesh for him. She had large, pendulous breasts and an ass he could only think of as majestic. He began to explore her with his mouth, and she sighed, spreading herself out for him.

He kissed his way down to the apex of her thighs, which was already fragrant and wet. Pressing his face to her, he worked avidly with his lips and tongue, at the same time reaching up to grab her large breasts.

"Oh, yes," she moaned, as he flicked his tongue and pinched her nipples, "yes, yes . . ." She bit her lip to keep herself from crying out louder, and possibly waking Davey. It would be extremely embarrassing to have the boy come looking for them, now.

She grabbed handfuls of the sheet on either side as Clint's mouth brought her to the brink of finishing. When he stopped, she grabbed for his head, but missed.

"Don't stop!" she pleaded.

"Oh, I'm not stopping," he told her. "I'm just chang-
ing position."

On his knees, still between her widely spread legs, he
looked down at the acres of pale, smooth flesh that lay
before him. Dark, bushy hair covered her pink pussy, and
dark, turgid nipples topped her breasts, which were so
heavy that, while on her back, they flopped to either side.

"What are you looking at?" she asked.

"You're beautiful," he said.

Suddenly self-conscious, she folded her arms across
her breasts.

"I'm getting fat in my old age."

"You're not fat or old," he said.

"Oh, shut up and fuck me," she said, grabbing for
him.

He slid atop her and let his hard cock glide into her
wet, steamy depths.

"Oh, oh, oh . . . my," she breathed as he began to
move in and out of her.

He leaned down, kissed her and said, "Shh, you'll
wake Davey."

She grabbed his face in her hands and said, "If you
want to keep me quiet, you'll have to keep kissing me."

Before he could respond, she pressed her mouth to
his and drove her tongue deep . . .

***

Henderson found Coyote in front of the whorehouse.

"Goin' in or comin' out?" he asked.

"Goin' in," Coyote said. "I didn't find out anything in the saloons."

"Neither did I."

"I thought the girls here might've heard somethin'," the half breed said.

"You might be right," Henderson said, "and we might find out more if we both question 'em."

"You are probably right."

They mounted the front porch and Coyote knocked on the door. A small girl in a filmy gown opened it and smiled at them.

"Ah, you brought a friend," she said. "Come in."

They entered and she closed the door.

"And which girl are you interested in tonight?" she asked Coyote.

Coyote and Henderson both smiled, and the half-breed said, "All of them."

Chapter Twelve

Maddy came back into her bedroom, wearing a robe, and closed the door behind her. That done, she dropped the robe to the floor and walked naked to the bed. Clint enjoyed every step she took toward him.

"Can you do me a favor before you get back in bed?" he asked.

She stopped and asked, "What's that?"

"Turn around and walk back to the door."

She frowned but did it. When she got there, she looked over her shoulder at him.

"Is there anything wrong?"

Looking at her beautiful ass Clint assured her, "Not a damn thing."

She turned, presenting him with a view of the front again. Her nipples were still hard from all his attention.

"You're a beautiful woman," he said. "Come back to bed."

She hurried to the bed, her large breasts bouncing with every step.

"How's Davey?" he asked, as she snuggled up next to him.

"Fast asleep."

"That's good," Clint said. "Tomorrow I'll send some telegrams to San Francisco, trying to locate his uncle."

"We'll be alone here when you go."

"I'll have someone else take the messages to the telegraph office."

"Who?"

"The sheriff should be able to help me with that," Clint said. "I'll send instructions for the key operator to bring the responses here."

"So," she said, "more poker with Davey?"

"Until he goes to bed again."

She reached for his penis and began to stroke it to fullness.

"Speaking of which . . ."

***

"Who?" Henderson asked.

The small girl who had answered the door stared at him from the other side of the bed. She was naked, her body gleaming with sweat from their exertions.

"The doctor," she said, "He comes here from time to time to see me."

"And this time he talked about the boy?"

"Well," she said, "the boy's family. The father was shot, and the mother burned to death."

"And the boy?"

"He mentioned that he examined him," she answered. "Apparently he's in shock and is blocking the incident out of his mind."

"So he can't say anythin' about it?"

"Not so far."

Henderson tried not to sound too anxious. He leaned back, placing his hands behind his head. He asked his next question a nonchalantly as he could.

"So where is he?"

***

Henderson rushed down the hall to the room he knew Coyote was in. He pounded on it with his fist until Coyote opened the door. He stood there, naked, his cock at full mast, still glistening from the saliva—or other liquid—from the whore he was with.

"What do you want?"

"We found the boy."

"Where?"

"Well, I don't know exactly," Henderson said, "but I know who does."

"Who?" Coyote asked.

"The town doctor," Henderson said. "We'll have to tell Jimbo, but we'll question the doctor tomorrow."

Coyote turned and looked at the fleshy, naked blonde on the bed, then looked back at Henderson.

"You tell him," the half breed said. "I'm not finished here."

"He'll wanna hear from both of us."

"You tell him you found out who knows where the boy is," Coyote said. "Tell him I found nothing."

Henderson looked at the blonde again, and she smiled at him and waved.

"All right," he said. "Go back to what you were doin'."

"I will," Coyote said. "I will see you in the morning."

"Yeah, right."

Coyote closed the door and Henderson went downstairs and out of the building.

***

He found Jimbo still in the saloon.

"Where's Coyote?" Jimbo asked.

"It don't matter," Henderson said. "I found out who knows were the boy's at."

"Well then," Jimbo said, "get yourself a beer and tell me."

Chapter Thirteen

Clint was getting ready to seat himself at the table for breakfast when the knock came at the door.

"I'll get it," he told Maddy.

She turned from the stove.

"I'll wake Davey."

They both left the kitchen. She went up the stairs and he to the front door of the house. He opened the door to allow the sheriff to enter.

"Glad to see you," Clint said. "Breakfast is almost ready."

They headed for the kitchen, saw Maddy coming down with the sleepy-eyed, Davey.

" 'mornin'. champ," Clint greeted him.

"Good-morning, Clint," the boy said. "I smell bacon."

"So do I," Caldwell said.

"Hi, Sheriff," Davey said, waving.

They all went to the kitchen, and Maddy saved her bacon before it burned. She dished out the breakfast, gave the two men coffee and Davey milk, then coffee for herself as she sat.

"How was poker last night?" Caldwell asked.

Clint almost took all my sticks," Davey said, "but I'm gonna get 'em back."

"That's the spirit," the lawman said. "This is a great breakfast, Maddy."

"I woke up late," she said, looking at Clint, "or it would've been better."

"It's fine," Clint said. "Sheriff, I need someone to take some telegrams to the telegraph office for me. We're going to try and find Davey's uncle, in San Francisco."

"Uncle Billy?" Davey asked.

"Right."

"Well," Caldwell said, "you scratch 'em out and I'll take 'em over."

"I thought you'd have somebody else who could do that."

"That's okay," the sheriff said, "I pass that office every day."

"I'll get them done after breakfast," Clint said.

They finished eating, and the lawman waited while Clint wrote out the telegrams.

"I'll get 'em right over there," Caldwell said, taking them from Clint.

"Ask the clerk to bring the replies here, will you?" Clint asked.

"Will do." the lawman said. "Thanks for breakfast, Maddy. See you later, Davey."

" 'bye, Sheriff."

Clint walked the man to the door.

"What are your plans if you locate the uncle?"

"I'll contact him. If he'll take the boy, I'll bring Davey to him."

"And if he doesn't want him?"

"What happens next might depend on Maddy," Clint said. "If she wants Davey, I don't think he'd mind. How are you doing tracking down the killers?"

"Nobody seems to know anythin'," Caldwell said. "Wilson didn't have any friends, but what acquaintances I found said they didn't know of any enemies."

"Everybody has somebody who's out to get them," Clint said.

"But enemies?" Caldwell asked. "Willing to kill?"

"People kill for all sorts of reasons," Clint said. "Profit, jealousy . . . for hire."

"So you think somebody hired these men to kill the Wilsons?"

"It's possible," Clint said. "If you can't find anyone in town who even disliked them, you'll have to cast a wider net with your investigation."

"Dislike is one thing," the sheriff said. "Hate's another, altogether. I'll see you later."

Sheriff Caldwell left the house. Clint went back to the kitchen, found Maddy cleaning up. Davey was gone.

"Where's Davey?"

"He went to his room," Maddy said, "but he's ready for poker when you are."

"I'll go and get him," Clint said, "after another cup of coffee."

***

Henderson met Coyote in the lobby of their hotel the next morning.

"Are you ready to work?" he asked.

"Yes," Coyote said, "I am ready."

"I hope you're not too worn out from last night," Henderson said.

"If anyone is worn out," the half breed said, "it's the girl who was with me."

Henderson ignored the remark.

"The doctor's name is Pegram," he said. "He's been the sawbones here for a lot of years."

"Then he should know everybody in town."

"That's what Jimbo said," Henderson replied. "Let's go find out."

Chapter Fourteen

Sheriff Caldwell left Clint's telegrams at the telegraph office and went to his own office. When he got there, he found Mayor William Townes waiting for him. The Mayor was in his sixties, and had been in office for twenty years.

"Good-mornin', Mayor," Caldwell greeted.

"Not so good, Sheriff," Townes said.

"What's wrong?"

"Doc Pegram's been killed."

"What?"

"Beaten to death in his office. He was found by his first patient this morning."

"Jesus!"

Townes moved closer to Caldwell, almost nose-to-nose.

"I want the killers found!"

"So do I," Caldwell said. "They may be the same ones who killed the Wilsons."

"What makes you say that?"

"They could have been looking for the Wilson boy, Davey," Caldwell said. "Thanks to the story that appeared in the newspaper."

"I don't care about the Wilsons," Towne admitted. "I want Pegram's killer or killers found."

"I know he was your friend, Mayor."

"For over twenty years."

"But to me the Wilsons are just as important, as is the boy."

"Whatever it takes, Sheriff," Townes said. "Whatever it takes!"

"Where's the body?"

"At the undertaker's."

The Mayor turned and stormed out.

Sheriff Caldwell did not even bother to sit down. He immediately left his office.

***

Clint was surprised to see the sheriff at the door.

"That was fast," he said, stepping out onto the porch

"Not so fast," the lawman said. "You've got to move the boy."

"Why?"

"Doc Pegram was found dead in his office this mornin'," Caldwell said. "He was beaten to death."

"You think he told someone where Davey is?"

"It's possible."

"We have to move Maddy, as well," Clint said. "We can't have her here alone if they show up."

"Good idea," Caldwell said. "I'll keep watch from here while you get them packed and ready to move."

"Right."

Clint rushed into the house, where Maddy and Davey were sitting on the sofa. Davey had a deck of cards in his hands.

"All right," he said, "we've got to pack and get out of here."

"What's wrong?" Maddy asked.

"Doc Pegrams been killed," Clint said. "We think he may have told someone where Davey is."

"Oh, God!" she breathed. She grabbed Davey's hand. "Come on, sweetie, we have to pack a few things."

"What's wrong?" he asked.

"I'll tell you while we pack," she promised, dragging the boy to the stairs.

Clint returned to the front door and kept watch with the lawman.

***

"You killed him, too?" Jimbo asked.

"Hey, he died," Henderson said. "He was an old man."

"Did you at least find out where the boy is?" Jimbo asked.

"Yeah, we did," Henderson said. "He's at the home of somebody named Madeleine Hinton."

"Do we know where that is?"

"We can find out."

"Then do it!" Jimbo snapped. "And do it without killin' anybody else!"

Henderson and Coyote left the saloon. Jimbo sat back in his chair, shaking his head.

***

Maddy didn't have much to pack for Davey, so when she came down she had two carpetbags, and two more things.

"Is that it?" Clint asked.

"That's all. I thought you'd want these." She handed him his rifle and saddlebags. Clint was surprised she had carried all of that down.

"Thanks," he said. He looked at Caldwell. "Anything?"

"Not yet."

"We better get moving, then," Clint said.

"To where?" the sheriff asked.

"I thought you'd have an idea," Clint answered.

63

Chapter Fifteen

"There's the house," Henderson said.

"It is a big one," Coyote said.

"Not big enough," Henderson said. "Come on."

They quickly closed the distance between them and the house. Deciding to take offensive action, Henderson simply kicked the front door in, and they entered.

"Check upstairs!" Henderson snapped.

By the time Henderson finished searching the downstairs, Coyote was coming back down the stairs.

"Nothing," he said.

"Nothing here, either," Henderson said.

"Do you think they knew we were coming?"

"Could be they're just out," Henderson said. "You stay outside on watch, in case they come back. I'll go and talk to Jimbo."

"Right," Coyote said.

They both left the house and split up outside. Coyote found a likely spot to watch the house from, while Henderson headed for town to talk to Jimbo.

***

Sheriff Caldwell finally came up with a suggestion as to where to take the boy and Maddy.

"My house," he said. "There's no one there."

When they reached the house, Clint saw that it was little more than a shack.

"This what the town gave you?" he asked.

"It suits me," Caldwell said. "After all, I live alone." He looked at Maddy.

"It'll do," she said. "We just have to keep Davey safe."

Caldwell unlocked the front door and allowed Clint, Maddy and Davey to precede him. The interior was small, and messy.

"I'm sorry about this," he said to Maddy. "I haven't had time to clean up."

"Don't worry," she said, looking around, "Davey and I will handle it."

"There's a bedroom," Caldwell said. "You and Davey can have it."

"But . . . where will you sleep?"

"Don't worry about me," he said. "All my cells are empty."

"And I'll sleep on the floor out here," Clint said. "Meanwhile, on your way back to your office would you tell the telegraph operator to bring you the replies?"

"I'll do that."

Sheriff Caldwell left.

"Well," Maddy said to Clint, "roll up your sleeves."

"What for?" he asked.

"You're going to help us clean this place up."

***

Jimbo sent Henderson to retrieve Coyote from in front of Maddy's house that afternoon.

"There's no point watchin' the house," he said. "Killin' that doctor made 'em move the boy, again."

"To where?" Coyote asked.

"That's what you two idiots are gonna figure out," Jimbo said. "And remember—"

"I know," Henderson said. "Don't kill nobody, this time."

As the two men left, Jimbo was thinking if they didn't find the boy this time, he was going to have to leave the saloon and do it himself.

He waved at the saloon girl for another cold mug of beer . . .

***

It took most of the morning and afternoon to get the little house clean enough to satisfy Maddy.

"Are we done, yet?" Davey asked for the tenth time.

"Yes, we're done," Maddy said. "I'm going to see what the sheriff has that I can make for supper."

As it turned out, there wasn't much.

"Clint," she said, "I have to go shopping."

"You can't," Clint said, "not by yourself."

"But if they're after anyone it's Davey, not me," she reasoned.

"If they find out that Davey was in your house, they're after both of you."

"Then you go."

"And leave you alone?"

"No one knows we're here," she said. "And you don't know that you've been connected to Davey. This house isn't even inside the town limits. But you can still walk and be back in no time, with some food for me to cook."

"Maddy—"

"We can't let the poor boy starve," she broke in. "There's a gun here. We'll be fine. Just pick a few things up at the mercantile."

Clint knew he shouldn't go, but Maddy was adamant.

"I'll make a quick trip," he said.

"That's all I ask."

Chapter Sixteen

"The Gunsmith?" Jimbo said.

"That's what we heard," Henderson said. "The Gunsmith is in town."

Jimbo gave that some thought.

"There ain't no guarantee there's a connection," he said, then. "Clint Adams is no lawman."

"We heard from somebody who knew the doctor," Henderson said. "It was Adams who brought the boy in."

"Damn!"

"Are you afraid of him?" Coyote asked.

"I'm not afraid of him," Jimbo said, "but I've got no desire to go against him."

"But, if you kill him—" the half breed started.

"I'm not looking for a reputation," Jimbo said. "The less people know about me, the better."

"So what do we do?" Henderson asked.

"Keep an eye out for Adams," Jimbo said. "If he's involved, he'll lead us to the boy. If he's not, we'll know about it soon enough."

"Right."

Jimbo looked at Coyote.

"Don't approach him, understand? If you want to make a run at the Gunsmith and his reputation, wait til I say so!"

"If that is what you want," Coyote said.

"That's what I want."

Henderson grabbed Coyote's arm and dragged him to the saloon doors.

Jimbo was thinking it might be time for him to get more involved. But first he had somebody to talk to. He stood and left the saloon.

***

Clint picked up everything on Maddy's list and got back to the house inside of an hour.

"See?" Maddy said, while unpacking the box he'd been carrying. "I told you you'd be back in no time." Davey was sitting on the floor, playing solitaire.

"I was worried the whole time," he said. "Hopefully there's enough supplies for a couple of meals."

"You think that'll be enough?"

"We should know in a couple of days if we've located Davey's uncle. Once we get the boy out of town, he should be safe. As for you . . ."

"Don't worry about me," Maddy said. "Once you and Davey are gone, I'll go back home. The sheriff will look in on me. Now go and keep him company while I make supper."

Clint walked over to the boy and asked, "Ready for some more poker?"

"Yeah!" Davey said, enthusiastically.

"Deal 'em out," Clint said, sitting cross-legged, across from him on the floor.

"Clint?" Davey said.

"Yeah?"

"Do you always wear your gun?"

"Yes, I do."

"Are you afraid someone is gonna take a shot at you?" Davey asked.

Clint decided to be truthful with the boy.

"Yes."

"Why?"

"Some people think it would be good for them if they killed me."

"But killing is bad."

"Yes, it is."

"Then why do they wanna kill you?"

"Davey," Clint said, "some men think it's important for them to have a reputation."

The boy screwed up his face.

"What's a . . . rep-a-tation?"

"That's when a man is considered to be famous."

"Famous?" Davey asked. "Like . . . like Wild Bill Hickok?"

"Yes," Clint said, "Wild Bill was famous."

"And somebody killed 'im!" Davey exclaimed. "Is that what ya mean?"

"Yes."

"And it made that person famous?"

"Yes, but for a bad reason," Clint said. "And the law made him pay for it."

"By puttin' him in jail?"

"Exactly." Clint didn't bother telling Davey that Jack McCall was executed for killing Bill.

"So if somebody kills you, they'll go to jail."

"But I always wear my gun to keep anybody from killing me."

"But what if *you* kill somebody?" Davey asked. "Will you go to jail?"

"No."

"Why not?"

"Because I only kill someone when they're trying to kill me."

Chapter Seventeen

Sheriff Caldwell stopped at the undertaker's office.

"He was beaten to death," the undertaker, Wendell Zack, said. "That's all I know. I ain't a doctor."

"Well, with Doc Pegram dead, you're the closest thing to it, we have," Caldwell said. "I wanna know if he was being tortured when he died."

"I'll look closely at the body, that's all I can do," Zack said.

"Thanks, Wendell. I'll be back in a while."

Zack nodded and the sheriff left.

***

Jimbo entered the man's office.

"What the hell are you doin' here?" The man immediately jumped up from his desk, checked to be sure his door was locked, then looked out the window. "Did anyone see you come in?"

"No, I was careful."

"Well," the man said, returning to his desk, "what is it?"

"First of all," Jimbo said, "you didn't tell me the Wilsons had a kid."

"He's an infant," the man said. "He won't be a problem."

"He's not an infant, and he might know somethin'."

"Then deal with it!"

"I'm tryin', but we can't find 'im. And it seems Clint Adams is the one who brought him to town."

"That's right," the man said. "He found the boy and his parent's bodies. He and the boy are at Madeiline Hinton's house."

"Not anymore," Jimbo said. "They've been moved." Jimbo sat.

"I didn't invite you to sit!" the man said.

"And you didn't tell me the Gunsmith was involved," Jimbo said.

"It's your job to kill, isn't it?" the man asked. "So kill him."

"Not for what you paid me," Jimbo said. "The Gunsmith is extra, a lot extra. If he's protectin' the boy, it's gonna be a problem."

"You get rid of the boy and the problem goes away," the man said.

"If Adams is involved, there's no dealin' with the boy without dealin' with him, too."

The man sat back in his chair with a sour look on his face.

"All right," he asked, "how much?"

"We'll negotiate," Jimbo said, "but first, how about offering your guest a drink?"

***

Sheriff Caldwell looked up from his desk as his office door opened. It was the telegraph key operator.

"Here are your replies, Sheriff."

"Thanks."

Caldwell took the three telegrams and the clerk left. For a moment Caldwell was tempted to read them, but in the end, he simply left his office to deliver them to Clint.

"Just in time," Maddy said, as he entered, "I just made a fresh pot."

"Sounds good."

Caldwell glanced over at Clint and Davey, playing poker on the floor. The amount of toothpicks in front of each of them looked even.

"I got your replies," he said.

Clint turned and said, "Great."

Caldwell handed them to him.

"You didn't read them?" Clint asked.

"No," Caldwell said, "they're yours."

Clint was impressed by the man's self-control.

"I'll be right back, Davey. This is about your uncle."

Clint stood, walked to the table, sat and began to read.

"Good news?" Maddy asked, looking over his shoulder.

"A friend of mine named Duke Farrell knows Davey's uncle," Clint said. "He's offered to go to the man and tell him about his brother, sister-in-law and nephew. He'll get back to me with the uncle's reaction."

"Any idea when?" Caldwell asked. "I'd like to get Davey out of town."

"So would I," Clint said, folding the telegrams.

Maddy put two cups of coffee on the table for the men.

"I'll keep Davey occupied while you two gents plan your next move."

"Thanks, Maddy," Clint said.

He watched as the woman went over and sat on the floor with the boy. The folds of her dress spread out around her. It was a simple dress, but she was lovely, nonetheless.

"I'll give you another telegram for Duke," Clint said. "I'll ask him to approach William Wilson about Davey."

"I didn't tell you," Caldwell said, while Clint wrote. "Pegram and the Mayor were old friends. The Mayor wants his killers."

"And the killers of the Wilsons," Clint added.

"He doesn't really care about them," the lawman said. "Or Davey. He just wants me to find the men who killed his friend."

"Just like a politician," Clint said. "Only worried about what he wants."

"Well," Caldwell said, "he's my boss."

"I get it," Clint said, handing him the new telegram. "You're looking for Doc Pegram's killer or killers. Only thing is, they're probably one and the same."

Chapter Eighteen

After Sheriff Caldwell left, Clint sat at the table with Maddy. She had told Davey to play solitaire while she and Clint talked. He collected the cards from the floor and dealt them out.

Clint told Maddy about sending another telegram to Duke Farrell. "We should know pretty soon if Davey's uncle will take him."

"I hope he will," she said. "The poor boy needs to be with family."

"Soon he's going to have to deal with the fact that he's lost his parents."

"If it hits him while he's still here, I'll help him," she said.

"I hope it doesn't hit him too hard."

"It's bound to," she said. "After all, he's just a little boy."

"He's quite a boy, though," Clint said. "It's too bad this had to happen to him."

"Are you going to find out who killed his parents?"

"That's the sheriff's job," Clint said. "Apparently, the same men killed the doctor. The Mayor's on his ass to find them."

"So you'll leave it to him?"

"He's the law. Besides, someone has to take Davey safely to his uncle."

"If his uncle takes him."

"Yes, there is that."

"Well," Maddy said, "like I told you before, if his uncle won't take him, I will."

"That might even be better for the boy," Clint said. "After all, you already love him."

"Yes, I do," Maddy said.

Maddy got up and poured Clint some more coffee.

"How long do you think it'll take your friend to find Davey's uncle?"

"Not long," Clint said. "Duke tends to know everyone in San Francisco. I'd give him a day."

"Then we need to pack for Davey," she said. "I can take care of that."

"I'm going to take my coffee and sit outside," Clint said. "Keep watch."

"But no one knows we're here."

"They might guess," Clint said.

"Then I'll call you in when supper is ready," she said.

"That'll be fine."

Clint took his coffee cup outside and sat in a rickety chair.

***

When Jimbo left the man's office, he had himself a new deal that he could live with. He just had to keep Henderson and Coyote from finding out how much more money he was getting.

He went back to the saloon he was using as his head-quarters. It was Kellog's smallest and least patronized saloon. For that reason they treated their only regular customer well. He had barely sat down when the saloon girl brought him a cold beer.

"Thanks," he said.

"Will your friends be comin' in?" she asked.

"I'm sure they will."

"Good!"

He hoped when Henderson and Coyote did come in, they would have some idea where the boy was hiding. Jimbo didn't like the idea of killing a kid, but it was better than having the kid identify them and sending them to the gallows. Besides, he was sure that Coyote would have no qualms about getting it done. He had hired the half breed precisely for his lack of morals.

***

If the doc was still alive, Sheriff Caldwell would have checked in with him on the condition of the newspaper editor, Mike Keller. But the doc was dead, and Keller was still in a bed at the doc's office. He was going to have to ask the undertaker to look in on him. If he came around, Keller might be able to identify the men who had beaten him. They had to be the same who had killed the doc, and the Wilsons. Caldwell didn't like the idea of killers walking around his town, free.

Caldwell's problem was that he wasn't a detective. The only way he might be able to catch the killers—and keep his job by making the mayor happy—was to wait for them to find Clint and Davey, and then make a try for them. That was a last resort, but one he might have to use before Clint left Kellog with the boy to take him to his uncle.

He didn't like the idea of using Clint and the boy as staked goats, but it could come to that.

First, he would have the undertaker look in on Keller and see if the newspaperman could tell them anything.

So he left his office and headed for the undertaker, Zack's.

Chapter Nineteen

Davey came running out of the house, yelling, "Supper's ready."

Clint almost shouted at the boy to get back inside, but stopped himself. Instead, he stood up.

"Let's get to it, then, champ." Later, he would have to explain to the boy that he couldn't be seen outside the house.

"Is the sheriff comin' for supper?" Maddy asked.

"I don't really know."

"Well," she said, "I made plenty if he shows up."

The three of them sat at the rickety table the sheriff used to eat on. Clint had to put something underneath one of the legs to even it out so the table wouldn't rock while they ate.

During supper Davey suddenly asked, "Are we gonna go see my Uncle Billy?"

Clint and Maddy exchanged a glance before he answered the boy.

"We're trying to see if we can find him," he said. "If we do, then we'll see."

"I hope we do," Davey said. "I ain't seen Uncle Billy since I was real little."

"Where was that, Davey?" Clint asked.

"At our house," he said. "He surprised us by showin' up at the door."

"And when was that?"

"I ain't sure," the boy said. "I think I was two."

That was three years ago.

"And you remember that?" Clint asked.

"I remember Uncle Billy was funny, but Mama wasn't laughing."

"Why not?"

Davey shrugged.

"I remember she said Uncle Billy was a bad man."

After supper Davey went back to his cards.

"How could he remember that?" Clint asked. "He was two years old."

"I don't know," Maddy said.

"It's . . . strange."

"If he remembers his mother said his uncle was a bad man, maybe—"

"Let's wait and see what my friend Duke says," Clint cut her off. "He's a good judge of character."

"Okay."

***

Jimbo watched as Henderson and Coyote approached his table. By the time they got there, the saloon girl set three mugs down.

"Thanks, honey," Jimbo said.

The two men sat down.

"Well?"

"No sign of 'im," Henderson said.

"Nothin'?" Jimbo asked.

Coyote shook his head.

"Nobody's seen the kid," Henderson said.

"What about the woman?"

"Folks know 'er, but ain't seen her for a day or so," Henderson said.

"They gotta be somewhere," Jimbo said. "Anybody seen the Gunsmith?"

"Yeah," Henderson said. "The clerk at the mercantile said he was in there earlier today, buyin' supplies."

"For travelin'?"

"Naw, not the kind you'd take on the trail," Henderson said. "Meat and eggs, some flour—"

"You could use that in a trail camp," Jimbo said.

"The clerk says he asked 'im," Henderson said. "Adams said he'd be in town a while."

"Okay," Jimbo said, "he's in town. Find 'im. He can't stay out of sight. Not a man like him."

"Why do we wanna mess with the Gunsmith?" Henderson asked.

"Because he'll lead us to the boy."

Henderson and Coyote looked at each other.

"You ever gonna leave this saloon?" Henderson asked.

"I sure am," Jimbo said, "as soon as you give me a reason to."

The two men looked at each other again, drank some beer, got up and left.

***

Clint watched as Maddy put Davey to bed, then came out of the room.

"Aren't you goin' to bed?" he asked.

"Not yet," Maddy said, giving him a look. "I wish we could . . . you know."

"I know," Clint said, "but this house is too small."

"Too small for a kiss?" she asked.

He reached out, drew her to him and kissed her.

"No," he said, "not too small for a kiss."

Caldwell had a threadbare sofa in the middle of the room. They sat on it close together and kissed some more. Then Maddy put her head on his shoulder and fell asleep.

Chapter Twenty

The next morning Sheriff Caldwell came to the house with Clint's reply telegram.

"That was fast," the lawman said. "The key operator caught me as I was walkin' past."

"I figure Duke would get it to me quick."

"Sit down for breakfast, Sheriff," Maddy said.

"Thanks, Maddy."

Clint unfolded the telegram and read it.

"What's it say?" Maddy asked.

"Duke says Bill Wilson is willing to take the boy," Clint said. "He also says Wilson's a gambler. He doesn't know what he'll do with a child."

"A gambler?" Maddy looked dubious. "With Davey's love of poker, Uncle Billy might turn him into a gambler, as well.

"But he's the boy's uncle," Clint said. "If he wants to take him . . ."

"So you'll take Davey to San Francisco?" she asked.

"We'll leave tomorrow," Clint said.

Maddy grabbed Clint's arm.

"If you meet this man, and you don't like him," Maddy said, "you bring the boy back here."

"Yes Ma'am."

Maddy nodded, called out, "Davey, breakfast," and started dishing it out.

***

After breakfast Clint stepped outside with the sheriff.

"When I leave, you'll keep looking for the killers, right?" Clint asked.

"I'll keep lookin', or the mayor will have my head."

"And you'll watch out for Maddy?"

"Definitely."

"Now, Davey and I will leave early, before first light, so we're not seen," Clint said, "But I'm going to travel as if we're being followed, just in case."

"Good idea," the lawman said.

"I need a favor, though," Clint said. "I need a horse for Davey."

"I'll bring one here," Caldwell promised. "I'll bring it after dark. Yours, too."

"Okay, good," Clint said.

"What about supplies?" the lawman asked.

"I'll travel light, pick some supplies up at the next town."

"Good enough," Caldwell said. "I'll see you out here tomorrow mornin', before first light."

"And sheriff," Clint said, as they man started to walk away.

"Yeah?"

"Watch your back," Clint said. "They beat Keller almost to death and killed Doc Pegram."

"It'll be a little harder to kill me," Caldwell said. "I guarantee it."

Clint waited til the lawman was out of sight, then turned and went back into the house.

***

Later Clint took Davey aside to talk to him.

"Davey, your Uncle Billy wants me to bring you to him in San Francisco."

"Really?" Davey asked. "And Aunt Maddy?"

"No, just you," Clint said.

"And when we get there, will you stay?" Davey asked.

"No," Clint said. "When we get there, you'll be with family, and I'll be on my way."

"Okay . . . I guess."

"Look Davey," he said crouching down and taking the boy by the shoulders, "is there any reason you don't want to go to your uncle? Tell me now if there is."

The boy thought and said, "No, Clint, I wanna go."

"Then we'll leave tomorrow morning," Clint said. "You go get some sleep."

"All right." The boy started walking toward the bed, then turned. "Do I get a horse?"

"Can you ride?"

"I can ride."

Clint smiled.

"Then you get a horse."

"All right!"

Maddy tucked Davey in, then came outside to stand with Clint.

"Are you going to sleep tonight?" she asked.

"No," he said. "There's no point in taking chances on our last night in town. I'm going to keep watch."

"Then I'll make you a big pot of coffee."

"Thanks."

She went back inside, and Clint stared out into the distance as dusk turned to dark.

Chapter Twenty-One

Clint was out in front of the house at five a.m. and heard the sound of horses approaching. Eventually, he spotted the sheriff leading his Tobiano and another horse.

"I figured this pony ought to be good enough for the boy," Caldwell said, as he reached the house.

"Looks good," Clint said.

"You plan on makin' the whole trip to San Francisco on horseback?"

"I figure anybody looking for us would be checking the trains," Clint said. "It may take longer to get there, but it'll be safer."

"It's up to you," Caldwell said.

"Is that my horse?" Davey asked from behind them.

Both men turned, saw the boy standing with Maddy.

"That's your horse, Davey."

"Wow." Davey looked up at Maddy. "My own horse."

The boy ran to the pony and stroked its nose.

"Does he have a name?" he asked.

"You name him, Davey," Clint said, "but think about it while we ride."

Clint grabbed the boy by the hips and lifted him up onto the horse.

"He's great!" Davey said, enthusiastically.

"You didn't say goodbye to me, Davey," Maddy said.

She walked to the horse and gave the boy a big hung.

"You mind what Clint says, you hear?" she said.

"I hear, Aunt Maddy."

Clint turned to the sheriff and shook hands.

"Good luck, Adams."

"You, too, Sheriff," Clint said. "I hope you find your killers."

"I will," Caldwell said, "that is, unless they follow your trail."

"Well," Clint said, mounting up, "hopefully leaving at this time will avoid that."

* * *

For a change, Henderson and Coyote found Jimbo in a café, rather than a saloon. They sat with him at his table, and they all had breakfast.

"Somethin' occurred to me, last night," Jimbo said.

"What's that?" Henderson asked.

"Adams may have left town," he said.

"What about the boy?" Coyote asked.

"If he left, he probably took the boy with him," Jimbo said.

"So they're gone," Coyote said. "We have nothing to worry about."

"The kid could still identify us."

"How?" Henderson asked.

"That stammer of yours, for one thing."

"I've been b-b-better lately."

"Yes, you have," Jimbo said. "Except maybe when you get upset."

"I'm t-t-tryin'."

"I'd like the two of you to look for the Gunsmith's horse."

"W-where?" Henderson asked.

"Where else?" Jimbo asked. "Livery stables. And see if anyone bought a horse."

Henderson looked at Coyote.

"We will try," the half breed said.

"Good," Jimbo said, "but go ahead and finish your breakfast first."

Henderson pushed his plate away and said, "I'm f-f-finished."

Coyote looked at his plate, shrugged, and stood up.

"We will get to it," he said.

Jimbo watched them leave, then took the remainder of the bacon from Coyote's plate.

***

"Now what?" Maddy asked the sheriff, after Clint and Davey were out of sight.

"I can see you safely home," he said.

She looked sad.

"The house is going to seem very empty, now."

The sheriff looked alarmed.

"You don't mean you want to stay here, do you?" he asked.

"No, no," she said, "don't worry. I'm leaving. Just give me time to pack."

"I'll wait out here," Caldwell said.

Caldwell was in a quandary as to what he hoped would happen. If the killers followed Clint Adams that meant they would leave town. There would be no more killing. But that wouldn't satisfy the mayor. He wanted Clint to find the killers and jail them.

But if they followed Clint Adams, there was a chance the Gunsmith would kill them, in defense of the boy. That would certainly satisfy the mayor.

"I'm ready," Maddy said, coming out with a carpet-bag in her hand.

"Do you know how to use a gun, Maddy?" the sheriff asked.

"I can shoot," she said, "but I don't own a gun."

"I'll get one for you, just in case. But let me get you home, first."

Chapter Twenty-Two

Davey rode pretty well for a five-year-old.

"I used to ride Willie," he explained.

"Who's Willie?"

"He was our plow horse," Davey answered. "I used to ride him bareback."

"That explains why you sit this horse so well," Clint said. "What've you decided to name him?"

"I'm gonna name him after our plow horse," Davey said. "I'll call him Willie."

"That's as good a name as any."

"Come on, Willie," Davey said. "Giddy-up."

They rode through the afternoon, with not one complaint from Davey, who didn't seem to tire. Clint kept a sharp eye on their back trail, but so far it didn't seem anyone was following them.

As it neared dark, Clint picked out a place for them to camp.

"Aw, do we hafta stop?" Davey asked. "I ain't tired."

"I am," Clint said, "and so are the horses. We'll camp, have supper, and get started again early in the morning."

"Oh, okay."

Clint usually had coffee and beans in his saddlebags. Since he hadn't restocked, he had enough for that night. They'd have to stop somewhere the next day for supplies.

Davey watched while Clint unsaddled the horses, tied them off so they wouldn't wander, then built a fire and made supper.

"Beans!" Davey said. "I like beans."

"You might not after a few days on the trail," Clint said, as they ate.

"Are we gonna be on the trail for a few days?"

"A lot of days, Davey," Clint said. "San Francisco is a long way off."

"How long will it take?"

"The better part of a month on horseback," Clint said. "Of course, we could hop a train at some point. I'll have to give it some thought."

"Clint?" Davey said, with a mouthful of beans.

"Yes?"

"Is somebody lookin' for me?"

"It's possible."

"Those men who killed my Ma and Pa?"

"Yes, Davey," Clint said, "They might think you can identify them."

"I didn't see them," Davey said, "but I heard them. Would that be good enough?"

"Probably not," Clint said. "But they don't know that."

Davey stopped chewing.

"You won't let them get me, will you?"

"Definitely not, Davey," Clint said. "Now finish your beans. We have to get some sleep."

***

Clint bedded the boy down, then returned to the fire to make a fresh pot of coffee for the night. He was going to stay awake, on watch, until he was dead sure no one was watching them. Then and only then would he bed down, himself, for a few hours.

He stared into the darkness, sipping coffee, wondering what Davey's Uncle Billy was going to be like? If the man was a gambler, what would he know about raising a child? Perhaps he was a gambler and was also a family man who would feel a responsibility toward his dead brother's son.

He would find out the answers, but first he had to get the boy there.

Satisfied that no one was out in the dark stalking them, he went to his bedroll and turned in.

***

If Clint had been alone, he would have had coffee for breakfast and gotten on the trail. But the boy needed to eat something, so he tossed some biscuits Maddy had given him into the pan to soften them up and gave them to Davey.

"Ain't you gonna eat somethin'?" the boy asked.

"I'm not hungry right now, Davey," Clint said. "We're going to stop at the next town and pick up supplies. We'll have some bacon with our beans tonight."

"Oh, boy!" Davey exclaimed. "Bacon and beans."

Clint had more coffee while the boy ate, then doused the fire and stowed the coffee pot and the pan in his saddlebags. When he saddled the horse, Davey stood by and watched.

"My Pa always told me to watch when people do stuff, and I'll learn," he said.

"Your Pa was a smart man."

Clint wondered how the boy could talk about his parents with no real emotion. According to Doc Pegram there was no telling when the shock would wear off and the reality of what happened would hit him. Clint wasn't looking forward to that, at all.

Chapter Twenty-Three

It was the day after Clint and Davey left town that Jimbo got the word.

"The hostler at the livery said the sheriff walked Adams' horse and one other out yesterday mornin', before light," Henderson said.

Jimbo pushed his breakfast plate away, still half-filled.

"Any idea where they were headed?" he asked.

"Not a clue," Henderson said. "But the sheriff asked the hostler for a horse gentle enough for a child to ride."

"Damn it!" Jimbo swore. "He's takin' that kid somewhere. Maybe to a U.S. Marshal."

"The kid didn't see us," Henderson said.

"We don't know that for sure," Jimbo said.

"The newspaper story said he was under the floor," Coyote pointed out.

"Speakin' of that, what's happenin' with that newspaper editor?"

"He ain't woke up yet," Henderson said, "maybe never will."

"If he does, he'll describe you two," Jimbo said. "It's just as well we get on the trail of Adams and the kid. Get us outfitted, Henderson."

"Right."

"Coyote, you're gonna track them."

"No problem," Coyote said.

"When are we leavin'?" Henderson asked.

"As soon as you get your ass outta here and get us outfitted!" Jimbo said.

Henderson and Coyote got up and left, while Jimbo went back to his breakfast, figuring it might be his last good meal for a while.

***

Sheriff Caldwell looked down at Mike Keller, still lying unconscious in a hotel bed, where he had been moved to after Doc Pegram was killed. There was no one in town with the medical experience to replace Doc Pegram, so the sheriff insisted undertaker Zack, look after him.

"I'm not used to taking care of live people, you know," Zack said.

"I just need someone to be here in case he comes to and talks."

"That's about all I can do," Zack said.

"Whatever happens," Caldwell said, "if he speaks, let me know what he says."

"I've got it."

Caldwell looked at his watch.

"I have to meet with the mayor," he said. "I'll see you later."

"Yeah, sure."

The sheriff left the hotel and went to City Hall.

"Anything?" the mayor demanded.

"No," Caldwell said, "Keller's still unconscious."

"And Adams and the boy?"

"They left town yesterday morning."

"What?" The mayor crashed his fist down on his table. "Why did you let them go?"

"I had no cause to hold them."

"You could have used that boy as bait."

Caldwell frowned.

"I wasn't gonna do that, mayor," he said. "I'll find Doc's killers another way—hopefully, when Mike Keller wakes up."

"And if he doesn't?"

"I'll figure somethin' out."

"You'd better!" the mayor said. "Don't forget, your job depends on this."

"Yeah, right," Caldwell said. "If I lose my job I lose that beautiful house, too."

He turned and walked out of the mayor's office.

When he got back to his own office, he found the hostler, Davis, waiting for him.

"What's on your mind, Davis?" he asked, seating himself behind his desk.

"I—I think I made a mistake, Sheriff," Davis said, scratching the grey hair on his head.

"Whataya mean?"

"Well," Davis said, "two men was askin' me about the Gunsmith's horse."

"What did you tell 'em?"

"I said you come for the horse and another one, and you left with the two of them yesterday mornin'."

"And they were interested in that information?"

"Real interested."

"Who were these fellas, Davis?"

"I dunno," Davis said. "Just a fella, and a half breed."

"A half breed?"

Davis nodded.

"The other fella did all the talkin'."

"Okay, Davis," Caldwell said, "Siddown."

Davis sat.

"Now you're gonna tell me what these two fellas looked like," Caldwell said, "and you're gonna describe them real good . . ."

Chapter Twenty-Four

Clint and Davey came to a small town called Adler. It had a bank, a saloon and, more importantly, a general store.

"Are we gonna stay here, Clint?" Davey asked.

"No, Davey," Clint said. "We'll get some supplies and then keep moving. There's plenty of daylight left."

"Good!" Davey said. "I wanna keep ridin' Willie." He rubbed the horse's neck.

"I tell you what," Clint said, dismounting. "You stay on your horse and hold onto mine. I'll be right back."

"Okay."

Clint didn't see harm in letting the boy wait outside. There was still no sign of anyone on their trail. He went into the general store, turned and realized he could still see the boy outside the door.

"Can I help ya, stranger?" the older man behind the counter asked. He was tall and thin, wearing a dirty white apron.

"I need a few things," Clint said, "Bacon, beans, coffee, and a couple of cans of peaches. Oh, and some of that hard candy."

"Comin' up."

The clerk collected all the items Clint wanted and added up the cost. Clint paid and carried the supplies outside in a canvas gunny sack.

"That's a big bag," Davey said. "Did you get anythin' for me?"

"Let's see," Clint said, sticking his hand in the bag, rooting around, and then coming out with a piece of candy.

"Yay!" Davey yelled, as Clint handed him the treat.

Clint closed the sack and tied it to his saddle.

"Did you get bacon, too?" Davey asked, as Clint mounted the Tobiano.

"Candy wasn't enough?"

Davey shook his head.

"I want bacon."

"You got it!" Clint promised. "We'll have bacon and beans tonight. Let's get moving."

They turned their horses and rode out of Adler.

***

Jimbo, Henderson and Coyote left Kellog before the hostler, Davis, could identify them to the sheriff. Jimbo had met with the man who had hired him and told him they would be on the trail of Clint Adams and the boy.

"Don't come back here," the man said, "ever. Let me know where you end up after you kill them, and I'll send your money."

"If you don't," Jimbo said, "I *will* be back here. Understand?"

"Perfectly."

Outside of town they stopped.

"How do we know w-which way they w-went?" Henderson asked.

"I've got some more information," Jimbo said. "Information you should have gotten."

"What's that?"

"Adams was exchanging telegrams with someone in San Francisco."

"Who?" Coyote asked.

"That doesn't matter," Jimbo said. "As long as we know that, we can figure he's headed there."

"So we're goin' to S-s-san Francisco?" Henderson said.

"We're headin' that way," Jimbo said. "If we keep movin' we'll catch up to him."

"What about t-trackin' him?" Henderson asked. "How's Coyote supposed to do that?"

"The hostler told you the sheriff picked up Adams' horse, and a smaller one, probably for the boy."

"I'll pick up those tracks," Coyote promised. "A small and larger horse, side-by-side." The half breed smiled. "That will be like a sign pointing in the right direction."

"There you go," Jimbo said. "And if we don't catch up to them on the trail, we'll find 'em in San Francisco."

"You're p-puttin' a lot of f-faith in your hunches," Henderson pointed out.

"My hunches, and Coyote's ability to read sign," Jimbo said. "You wanna stay behind and wait for that newspaperman to wake up and identify you?"

"No, no," Henderson said, "I'm c-comin' along. If only for the chance to kill the Gunsmith."

"Good," Jimbo said. "I'll take care of the kid, and you two can handle the Gunsmith."

"That will suit me, as well," Coyote said.

Jimbo looked behind, then ahead of them.

"Then let's ride west," he said, "and take it at a good pace."

"We have good animals beneath us," Coyote said. "We will catch them."

"If they're headin' for S-s-san Francisco," Henderson said.

"Shut up," Jimbo snapped.

Chapter Twenty-Five

As promised, when they camped for the night Clint made Davey bacon and beans. They sat at the fire and devoured the meal, washing it down with coffee and water.

"I like to drink milk with my supper," Davey pointed out.

"Well, we can't have milk on the trail, so you'll have to wait til we get to San Francisco for that."

"What's San Cisco like, Clint?" Davey asked.

"It's very big and very busy," Clint answered.

"That sounds scary," Davey said.

"There's lots for a boy to do there, Davey," Clint said. "You'll like it."

"I liked our house," Davey muttered.

"I know you did," Clint said, "but you know it's gone, don't you?"

Davey lowered his head.

"Yes," he muttered.

Clint wondered if he should also point out that Davey's parents were gone but decided against it.

"Can I have some more bacon?" the boy asked.

"Of course."

He put the rest of the bacon on the boy's plate, then sat back and watched him eat.

***

Jimbo and Henderson watched Coyote examine the ground.

"There's somethin' I've never been able to do," Henderson said. "Read the ground."

"It helps that he's half Apache," Jimbo said.

The half breed got down on one knee, stared at the ground, then lifted his head and looked ahead. Eventually, he stood and walked to where Jimbo and Henderson were waiting.

"I have them," he said.

"Are you sure?" Jimbo asked.

"Two horses, one smaller than the other. Looks like it might be a pinto."

"And?"

"And heading west," Coyote said.

"Yes."

"How far ahead of us?"

"Two days."

"Can we catch up to them in less than that?" Jimbo asked.

"That depends."

"On what?"

"On how hard we ride," Coyote said, "how hard they ride, whether or not they stop in a town for the night."

"Then we better get movin'," Jimbo said. "I don't want this to take forever."

They mounted their horses and Coyote took the lead.

***

Clint watched Davey sleep, while keeping watch. He didn't see anyone behind them, and more importantly, didn't feel anyone. He often put more confidence in what he could feel over what he could see, but so far, neither one was clicking in.

He poured a last cup of coffee before turning in, sat with his rifle across his legs. One thing he did have a feeling about was the boy. Davey seemed to be getting closer and closer to reacting to the death of his parents. First the mention of the old plow horse, Willie, then of the house he shared with his Ma and Pa. Perhaps the breakdown Clint had been waiting for was coming next. He actually hoped it didn't come while they were on the trail. San Francisco would be much better, where he could get the boy to a doctor if the need arose.

Davey whimpered in his sleep, turned over, but didn't wake. Clint finished his coffee and went to his bedroll.

***

Clint treated them both to more bacon for breakfast. The biscuits Maddy had given them were gone and Clint wasn't prepared to spend the time making more.

Davey kicked the fire cold, as Clint had decided to teach the boy some things while they were together. He was too small to saddle the horses, but breaking camp was a different matter. Clint allowed the boy to stow their gear in the saddlebags. He double-checked and found that the boy had done an admirable job.

"Okay," Clint said, "let's mount up."

As they rode, Clint instructed the boy on the proper way to travel, what to look out for—chuckholes, rattlesnakes, etc.—and keeping a wary eye out for trouble, such as bandits or Indians.

Davey had questions, all of which Clint answered, since they had nothing to do with his dead parents. Clint was waiting and dreading those questions, which he knew would come soon enough. Eventually the lad was going to want to know why his parents were killed. Clint was counting on Sheriff Caldwell to come up with those answers. He felt it was more important for him to get Davey safely to his uncle, than helping the law find their killers. The mayor was apparently on his back about finding the doctor's killer, and they were probably the same.

Chapter Twenty-Six

It soon became evident to Clint that Davey would not be able to make the entire trip on horseback. Each evening they camped, the boy seemed more and more tuckered out. In addition, the pinto the boy was riding was starting to drag its hooves. He changed their direction slightly, heading northwest to Amarillo, where he figured they could catch a train to San Francisco.

As they approached Amarillo, he continued to study their back trail for pursuers. He didn't see any but, sure enough, he started to get an itch at the base of his spine.

As usual, his feeling turned out to be right . . .

***

To the south, about a day behind, Jimbo and Henderson watched Coyote read sign, as they had become accustomed to doing.

"I think he d-drags this out," Henderson said, "tryin' to make it look h-h-harder than it is."

"If you think it's not that hard, you do it," Jimbo said.

Henderson drank from his canteen and said, "Naw, that's all r-right. Let 'im have his fun."

Coyote looked over at them and said, "He's headin' for Amarillo."

"What makes you say that?" Jimbo asked.

The half breed pointed.

"Straight line takes us right there," he said.

"Why Amarillo?" Henderson asked.

"That is easy," Coyote said, standing up. "The railroad."

"You think Adams is gonna take the railroad?" Jimbo asked. "I was thinkin' he was gonna ride all the way."

"He may have intended to do that," Coyote said, mounting his horse, "but the horse the boy is riding is starting to tire. And I would say the boy is also tiring."

"He's gonna put some distance on us if he catches a train," Henderson said.

"We'll catch the one after him," Jimbo said. "We'll make up the time."

"I do not like trains," Coyote said. "Men ride horses."

"You don't have to come," Jimbo said. "You can take your chances, leaving Adams and the kid alive."

"Even if the boy can identify us, he does not know our names," Coyote pointed out.

"And don't forget the newspaper editor," Jimbo said. "He'll give a good description of both of you."

"We should've k-killed him before we left," Henderson said.

Jimbo wasn't worried because the man could only describe Henderson and Coyote as his assailants.

"All right, then," Jimbo said. "Amarillo it is."

"Are we goin' all the w-way to S-s-san Francisco?" Henderson asked.

"If we have to."

"I ain't never been there," Henderson said.

"It sounds too big," Coyote said. "Too many people."

"I've been there once. Lots of beautiful women," Jimbo pointed out.

Coyote's eyebrows went up.

"Maybe it won't be so bad," he commented.

"After we take care of Adams and the kid, you can find out," Jimbo said.

"It's soundin' b-better already," Henderson said.

***

When they rode into Amarillo, Davey's eyes went very wide.

"It's so big!" he said.

"Yes, it is," Clint said. It was even bigger than he remembered.

Clint rode directly to the Southern Pacific railroad ticket office and learned the next train out was not until morning.

Out in front of the office he said to Davey, "We'll stay in a hotel tonight and have a good meal."

"Yay!"

"And maybe a bath."

"Aw!"

"But we'll start by bedding our horses down."

Clint chose a hotel near the railroad station and then a livery near the hotel. They arranged with the hostler to have the horses ready to travel early the next morning.

They walked to the hotel, Clint carrying his rifle and saddlebags.

"Can I get my own room?" Davey asked, as they entered.

"No," Clint said, "I think there's enough space for us to share one room."

"Aw."

Clint registered, explaining they would need a room for one night, only.

"And we'll be checking out to catch a train," he told the clerk.

"As you wish, Sir," the clerk said, handing Clint his key. "Have a pleasant night."

When Clint unlocked the door, Davey ran in and bounced on the bed.

"Yay!" he yelled.

"Okay, that's enough," Clint said, and the boy stopped. "Let's go and get something to eat."

"I'm hungry," Davey said. "Can I have steak?"

"We'll both have steak," Clint said. "And if you're really good, maybe no bath."

Davey looked excited and yelled, "Yaaaaaay!"

Chapter Twenty-Seven

Clint decided to eat in the hotel dining room, which looked decent. He ordered steaks for both of them, cut half of Davey's up for him, then put the other half on his own plate. He was quite hungry, himself.

The boy ate his meat and potatoes, but did not like peas, so Clint took those, too.

"This is really good," Davey said.

"Glad you're enjoying it."

"Can we have dessert?"

"Sure," Clint said. "What would you like?"

"Pie!"

"What kind?"

Looking more excited Davey snapped, "Rhubarb."

"Really?" Clint hated rhubarb.

"I love it!"

The waiter came over and Clint said, "Two pieces of pie, rhubarb and peach."

"Coming up, Sir," the waiter said. "Are you finished?"

"I'm still working on mine," Clint said. "He's finished."

The waiter took Davey's plate and said, "I'll be right back with the pie. Coffee? Milk?"

"Yes, and yes," Clint said.

While waiting for the pie, Clint finished his steak. It was okay, but not "good," as Davey said. Clint decided to get the boy a real good steak when they got to San Francisco. He knew of a half dozen fine restaurants in Portsmouth Square and the Barbary Coast.

The waiter came with their pie and drinks, and he took Clint's plate. Clint noticed two men across the floor paying attention to them. Was it possible the killers had caught up to them?

Davey attacked his pie. Clint cut into his but kept his eyes on the men in the room.

"This is good."

"Rhubarb," Clint said.

Davey suddenly stopped eating and a faraway look came into his eyes. Clint wondered if this was the moment the reality was going to hit the boy.

"Davey," Clint said, "finish your pie. We have to go to our room."

He stared at Clint, then slowly began eating his pie again. Clint wondered if rhubarb was his favorite because his mother used to make it, and if, for a moment, the boy was on the verge of an emotional breakdown.

He wondered if he should have Davey examined by a doctor before getting on the train? Or, by not doing so, was he risking a full-blown breakdown while they were riding the rails.

"I'm finished," Davey said.'

"Drink all of your milk."

"Yes, Sir."

Davey lifted his glass and drank down the remainder of his milk.

"Done!" Davey said, wiping his mouth with the back of his hand.

Clint stood up with Davey, while keeping one eye on the two men watching them. As they left the dining room and entered the lobby, the men stood and followed.

"Okay, Davey," Clint said, "I want you to get behind the front desk with the clerk."

"Really? Oh, boy!"

"And don't come out until I get you."

He walked the boy to the desk.

"Sir?" the clerk said.

"Keep this boy behind the desk, please."

The clerk, a young man in his twenties, looked surprised.

"Uh, but, for how long?"

"I'll let you know."

Clint turned away from the desk to face the two men who had followed them out.

"Stay right there."

The two men stopped and put their hands into the air. It didn't look as if either of them was armed. They were both in their thirties, and well dressed.

"Whoa," one of them said, "don't shoot."

"I'm not going to shoot," Clint said, "as long as your hands remain empty."

"We don't have any guns," the other said.

"Open your jackets."

Both men obeyed, showing themselves to be un-armed.

"Okay," Clint said, "arms down. Who are you and why are you following me?"

"You *are* the Gunsmith, right?" one asked.

"It's him, all right," the other one said. "I recognize him."

"Who *are* you two?"

"We're newspapermen," one said. "We were just havin' a bite to eat and recognized you."

"Can we do an interview? What are you doin' in Amarillo? Why do you have a little boy with you?"

"All of that is none of your business," Clint said. "And I don't do interviews."

"But—" one started.

"Go . . . away."

"Mr. Adams—" the other began.

"Now!"

Both men stepped back.

"Um, yes, okay," one said, grabbing the other one's arms. "Let's go."

He pulled his partner back. They both turned and walked away.

Clint turned to Davey and the clerk.

"Okay, let's go," he said to the boy.

"That's it?" the clerk asked.

"That's it," Clint said. "Thank you."

"Yes, Sir."

Davey came around the desk and they walked upstairs to their room.

Chapter Twenty-Eight

Clint was glad the men had turned out not to be two of the killers. He would have hated to have to kill them right in front of Davey.

"All right," Clint said, "time for bed."

"Aw, already?" Davey said. "Can't we play some cards?"

It was actually pretty early, even if they had to get up for an early train.

"All right," Clint said. "Let's play poker for an hour. But then we go to sleep. Deal?"

"Deal!"

***

"If we ride through the night, we can be in Amarillo by mornin'," Jimbo said.

"There are three of us," Coyote said. "If we ride through the night, it is likely one of our horses will step in a chuckhole. So we camp."

"If we camp, we might miss Adams and the kid," Jimbo said.

"You are the one who said we can catch the next train after them," Coyote said. "But we can only do that if we get there safe."

"He's r-r-right, Jimbo," Henderson stammered.

"Shut up!" Jimbo snapped. He looked at Coyote. "What if I insist?"

"Then you go ahead," Coyote said. "Henderson and I will come at first light."

Now Jimbo glared at Henderson, who looked away.

"All right," Jimbo said, giving in. "Coyote, make camp. Henderson, see to the horses."

"R-r-right," Henderson said.

Jimbo dropped his bedroll and sat on it, fuming. He was angry because Coyote was right. Having a horse break its leg would have put them even further behind the Gunsmith and the boy. They were going to have to catch up to them in San Francisco—which was a place Jimbo hated. He had been there once and swore never to go back.

By the time they reached San Francisco, it was going to be a pleasure to kill Adams and the kid.

He realized somebody was standing in front of him.

"Coffee," Coyote said.

Jimbo accepted the cup and said, "Thanks."

"Here." Coyote produced a bottle of whiskey and poured some into Jimbo's coffee.

"Thanks," Jimbo said, again.

Coyote went to the fire to prepare a mess of beans.

"How is he?" Henderson asked.

"He is all right," Coyote said. "We will catch up to Adams in San Francisco."

"I h-h-hope so," Henderson said.

He watched as Coyote heated the beans.

"Hey," he said, "when we catch 'em, who's gonna k-k-kill the k-k-kid?"

"I don't know," Coyote said. "It will depend on what happens when we get there."

"I-I d-don't know if I can do it."

"You didn't have any trouble with the mother," Coyote said. They had all taken turns raping the woman before killing her.

"That was an adult," Henderson said. "This is a kid."

"Then Jimbo will kill him, or I will," Coyote said. "The beans are ready."

"J-Jimbo, beans!" Henderson shouted.

Jimbo came over to the fire and the three of them ate their beans and drank coffee.

***

Clint was happy to see that Davey slept through the night and was still asleep in the morning.

"Come on, big boy," Clint said. "Time to get up."

Davey opened his eyes and rolled over.

"Clint?"

"Yup," Clint said. "Come on, time to get up."

Davey sat up and rubbed his eyes.

"Can we have breakfast?"

"There's no time," Clint said. "We'll have to eat on the train."

"Eat on the train?" Davey said, excitedly jumping out of bed. "Oh, boy! Come on, let's get dressed."

***

Clint got the horses settled in the stock car, then took Davey into the passenger car.

"When can we eat?" Davey asked.

"Let's give the train time to get going," Clint said. "We'll just get some seats now."

Clint found two seats, and let Davey sit by the window. As the train started moving, the boy couldn't take his eyes from the passing scenery.

Chapter Twenty-Nine

"Wow, look!" Davey said.

Sometime later, they were sitting in a dining car. While others were having lunch, Clint and Davey were eating a late breakfast. Davey was chewing and looking out the window at some cows.

Davey bit into his bacon and said, "This is good."

"Yes, it is." Clint also had a plate of bacon-and-eggs in front of him.

A woman sitting at a table across the way was watching them and smiling. Clint smiled back. At that point she leaned over.

"You and your son are so sweet together," she said.

"Thank you," Clint said, "but he's not my son."

"Clint's my friend!" Davey said.

"I see," she said. "Um, do you mind if I join you?"

"Please do," Clint said, standing.

The woman only had a cup of tea in front of her. She picked it up and stood. Clint hurried to block her progress momentarily.

"Davey's parents were killed recently," he said to her. "I'm taking him to his uncle in San Francisco. Please, don't mention his parents."

"I won't," she promised. "Thank you for telling me."

The woman sat opposite Davey as Clint sat back down next to the boy.

"My name's Laura Dickinson," she told them.

"My name's Clint Adams, and this is Davey," Clint said.

"Davey, you're so cute," she said. "You remind me of my own son when he was your age."

"Where is your son?" Davey asked. "I can play with him."

"He's not with me on this trip," she told him. Clint thought the woman looked momentarily sad. Oddly, the sadness made her even more lovely. She was dressed for travel in a gray suit, her auburn hair tucked behind her head, revealing a long, graceful neck.

As Clint watched, she and Davey fell into a conversation about what they were seeing outside the window. Clint called a waiter over and got Laura some more tea.

After a while, Clint looked around and said, "I suppose we should let someone else have this table."

"Do you have a sleeping cabin?" she asked.

"No, we have seats in the passenger car."

"If you'd like Davey to have a nap, he can do it in my car," she said. "He could even spend the night in my bunk."

"I might take you up on that later, so he can get a good night's sleep. But where would you sleep?"

"I'll sit in his seat, and we can get acquainted."

"I don't think I'd like to leave him alone," Clint said.

"That's sweet," she said. "Well, there are seats in my car. He could look out the window and we could get acquainted, there."

"I think that sounds like a good idea."

"We can go now," Laura said.

As they rose, Clint found himself slightly leery of Laura Dickinson's interest. Was it possible she was connected to the killers who were looking for them? Was this a trap to get him and Davey into her cabin? But the woman seemed sincere in her liking for Davey, so Clint decided to simply be ready for anything.

They walked to the car with the cabins, and he waited while she unlocked hers. She went in first and he followed, ready to grab his gun if need be. As it turned out, there was no one there, and Clint ended up feeling slightly paranoid.

After a pleasant afternoon of getting to know one another, the three of them went back to the dining car for supper. By the time they were done, Davey was yawning mightily. The rocking motion of the train was putting the boy to sleep.

***

When they returned to the cabin, Laura turned the bunk down and helped Davey off with his shoes. No sooner had the boy's head hit the pillow, he fell fast asleep.

"He's tired," she said.

"Yes," Clint said. "The plan was to make San Francisco on horseback, but I could see he was getting tuckered out."

"That's where his uncle is?" she asked.

"Yes."

She looked over at Davey to be sure he was asleep.

"What happened to his parents?"

"They were killed."

"Oh, God, by who?"

"We don't know," Clint said. "They hid Davey in a root cellar. He didn't see the killers, but he heard them. And then they burned down the house."

"Oh, God! The poor boy. How did he come to be with you?"

"I heard the shots and saw the smoke, then found Davey sitting on the ground next to his father's body."

"And his mother?"

"She was inside the burning house," Clint said. "I'm fairly certain she was already dead when it was torched."

"Oh," she said, her eyes tearing up, "I just want to wake him and hug him."

"And where's your son?"

She wiped tears from her eyes.

"He died," she said. "He was eight when he became ill."

"I'm so sorry," Clint said.

"It was some time ago," she said. "I was a very young mother."

"And his father?"

"He left town soon after he heard that I was pregnant," she said. "My son, Aaron, never met his father."

Clint looked over at Davey.

"These two boys have had hard young lives," Clint said.

"Davey looked so tired to me, I just wanted to help."

"I appreciate it," Clint said.

"I'm from the east, Clint," she said, "going west to try and start again. "I have to tell you, your name sounds familiar. Should I know who you are?"

"Not really," Clint said. "As Davey said, he and I are friends."

She would discover who he was soon enough, but he didn't want to deal with the questions, now.

Chapter Thirty

Clint and Laura talked for a few hours before they both got sleepy and drifted off. At one point Clint realized that Laura's head was on his shoulder, but didn't mind and drifted back to sleep. He jerked awake several times when he heard someone walking by outside the cabin, but then went back to sleep, again.

When Clint woke for good, the sun was coming up. Laura was still resting on his shoulder, and Davey was still fast asleep. As if sensing he was awake, Laura stirred and opened her eyes.

"Oh," she said, sitting up quickly, "I'm so sorry."

"For what?" Clint asked. "For giving me a more pleasant night than I expected?"

She covered her face with her hands.

"I must look terrible," she said. "I'm going to freshen up. Shall I bring back coffee?"

"That sounds good," he said. "When Davey wakes, we'll take him for breakfast."

"Good," she said, standing. "I'll be right back."

She left the cabin, closing the door firmly behind her. Clint couldn't help but wonder again if there was a plan afoot to take him unawares, which was never going to happen. Laura could have been completely innocent, only wanting to help, but Clint was still going to stay alert for anything.

"Clint?" Davey said sleepily from the bunk.

"Good morning, champ."

"Where's Mrs. Dickinson?" he asked, sitting up and rubbing his eyes.

"She went to freshen up," Clint said.

"When's breakfast?"

"As soon as she gets back," Clint said, "And you better remember to thank her for her bed."

"Where did she sleep?"

"In one of these seats," Clint said, pointing.

"With you?" Davey asked, eyes wide.

"Next to me," Clint said. "Come on, let's get your shoes on."

Clint was pulling the second one on when Laura reappeared, carrying coffee, tea, and milk.

"Hey, you're awake!" she said, with a big smile. Clint thought she had done an admirable job of freshening up.

"When's breakfast?" Davey asked.

"Davey," Clint said.

"Oh, yeah," the boy said, "thanks for the bed. When's breakfast?"

"Drink this milk and then we'll go," she said.

Davey hurriedly drank the milk down, half of it running down his chin.

"Now I have to clean you up," she said. "Clint, why don't you get us a table and we'll be along."

"That's all right," Clint said. "I'll wait."

He wasn't about to leave Davey alone with anyone, even Laura.

***

Once Davey was dry and clean, they walked together to the dining car. Clint and Davey ordered bacon-and-eggs, while Laura ordered tea and toast.

"That's all you're havin'?" Davey asked.

"I'm a woman, Davey," she said. "I have to watch my figure."

"But you're pretty!" Davey said. "Ain't she pretty, Clint?"

"She's very pretty, Davey."

"Well," Laura said, "I thank both you gentlemen."

While they ate, Davey asked Clint when they would be arriving in "San Cisco."

"Some time tonight, Davey," Clint said. "It'll be pretty late, and we'll get to a hotel as soon as possible."

"Which hotel?" Laura asked.

"I don't know, yet. My friend Duke Farrell has a hotel, but it's also a casino. I don't think it would be a good idea to take Davey there. We'll probably stay someplace outside of Portsmouth Square, away from Chinatown and the Barbary Coast."

"Wow," Laura said, "you're eliminating all the interesting places."

"Interesting to an adult," Clint reminded her, "not to a child. I'm thinking about taking Davey to the zoo."

"What's a zoo?" Davey asked.

"A place that has a lot of animals for you to look at," Clint said.

"And to pet," Laura added.

"Yay!" Davey said.

"I'd love to go with you guys when you do go," she said.

"We don't want to take up too much of your time," Clint said.

"Oh, I have loads of free time," she said, "believe me."

"Then it's a date," Clint said. "Right Davey?"

"Yeah, right!"

"I'm looking forward to it."

Davey put a big piece of bacon into his mouth, chewed it, swallowed it, then said, "Clint, what's a date?"

Chapter Thirty-One

It was late when the train pulled into San Francisco because of an explosion in the engine, and the need to make an emergency stop for water.

"Okay, champ," Clint said, "we'll need to get the horses off, and then find a hotel."

"Clint," Laura said, "why don't you let me take Davey to my hotel and put him to bed while you get your horses and your rooms."

"No, that's okay, Laura," Clint said. "I'll keep the boy with me."

"Wow," she said, "you really are protective of him."

"The men who killed his parents might be looking for him," Clint said.

"Why?" she asked. "To kill him?"

"Yes."

"A little boy?"

"A little boy who might identify them," Clint said, "and might send them to the gallows."

"Oh my God," she said, "no wonder you won't let him out of your sight."

"Not for a second," he said.

"But . . . you can't trust me?"

"We just met, Laura," Clint said. "No offense."

"I'll try not to take any," she said. "But listen, I'm going to my hotel now. The Billingham, outside of Portsmouth Square. When I get there, I'll register you and Davey, that way you can get him right to bed."

"Thanks very much, Laura."

"I'll see you in the morning for breakfast."

"In the lobby," Clint said. "Got it." He put his hand on Davey's shoulder. "Let's go get our horses, champ."

***

Clint walked the Tobiano and Davey's pony out of the stock car, and they rode them to the Billingham Hotel. It was a notch below Portsmouth Square hotel, but still quite impressive. As promised, Laura had a room waiting for them. The clerk said they're horses would be taken care of.

Clint accepted the key and walked Davey to the room, which was actually a two-room suite.

"Wow," Davey said, "which is our room?"

"Both of them," Clint said. "This whole thing is our room."

They left the sitting room and entered the bedroom.

"Two beds? One's mine?" Davey asked, wide-eyed.

"One's yours," Clint said.

"Which one?"

"You pick," Clint said.

"I want this one," Davey said, jumping on the bed furthest from the door.

"Good," Clint said. "Let's unpack and get you in your pajamas."

When Clint tucked Davey into bed, the little boy closed his eyes and immediately fell asleep. Clint went out to the sitting room and sat in an overstuffed chair. In the morning he would have to change rooms. He wasn't prepared to pay for a two room suit in San Francisco. Apparently, Laura was a well-to-do lady. Also, in the morning he was going to have to go and see Duke Farrell and find out where Davey's Uncle Billy was.

He realized he was dog tired when he jerked awake in the chair. Making sure the door and windows were locked, he went into the bedroom and climbed under the covers of his own bed, while Davey slept peacefully in his.

***

When they got down to the lobby the next morning, they found Laura waiting for them.

"Good-morning, gentlemen," Laura greeted. She was wearing a green suit that was identical to the grey one she had worn on the train.

"Good-morning, Miss Dickinson," Davey said.

"Davey, you can call me Laura."

"Can I call you Aunt Laura?" he asked.

She crouched down in front of him and said, "I'd be honored if you'd call me Aunt." She hugged him.

She stood up and said to Clint, "Let's go in and eat. The food here is very good."

"Let me go to the desk first," Clint said. "I have to change rooms."

"Change? Why?"

"We're in a two-room suite," Clint said. "I can imagine what that must be costing."

"It's costing you nothing," she said.

"How is that?"

"The owner has arranged for you to have the suite free," she said.

"How did that happen?"

"Easy," she said, with a beautiful, broad smile. "I'm the owner."

"What?" Clint was shocked.

Chapter Thirty-Two

They went into the dining room, got a table, and ordered breakfast before they continued talking.

"This is what I decided I was going to do when I came west," Laura said. "I bought this hotel."

"So you're . . ."

". . . rich? Yes, I am. Are you going to hold that against me?"

"No, I'm not. And me being who I am had nothing to do with us getting the suite?"

"Oh, no," she said. "I mean, I thought your name was familiar."

"But you know I'm Clint Adams, the Gunsmith, right?"

"I realized it after you and Davey spent the night in my cabin," she said. "But it's got nothing to do with the suite, believe me. Word that the Gunsmith is at the Billingham is not going to get out."

"I hope not."

"Clint," she said, "I'd like you to begin trusting me."

"If the word *doesn't* get out, that will go a long way towards that happening."

"Good," she said, "because I want you to be my guests as long as you're here in San Francisco."

"But . . . why?"

"Because this little boy," she said, indicating Davey as he consumed his breakfast, "deserves to be happy."

"Yes, he does."

"And you're a wonderful man to make him your responsibility."

"I found the boy sitting by his dead father," Clint said, "and he needed help. Anyone would've done the same."

"I don't think that's true," she said. "Allow me to keep thinking you're a wonderful man."

"That's fine," Clint said. "Think what you want, and thank you for the hospitality."

"You're quite welcome. It's all free—the room, and the food."

"Yay, free," Davey said. "When do we go to the zoo?"

"I'll get you tickets for that," Laura said.

"That's good, but not today," Clint said.

"Aw, why not?" Davey asked.

"Because, champ," Clint said, looking at the boy, "today we're going to find your Uncle Billy."

***

After breakfast Clint and Davey went to Portsmouth Square to see Duke Farrell. When Clint went to Farrell's hotel, he found that the man had moved to a larger one. Business must have been very good for Duke.

The new hotel and casino was called simply DUKE'S. Clint took Davey into the high-ceilinged lobby and approached the front desk.

"Sir?" the bow-tied clerk said.

"I'd like to see Duke."

"Mr. Farrell is a busy man," the clerk said. "Can I say who's calling?"

"Clint Adams."

The man's stuffy attitude changed suddenly, and he smiled.

"Mr. Adams. Of course, Mr. Farrell is waiting for you and your little friend. This way."

The clerk came around from behind the ornate front desk and led the way down a corridor. When they reached a closed door, he knocked and opened it.

"Mr. Farrell, Mr. Adams and his friend are here."

"Well, bring them in, damn it!"

"Go right in, Mr. Adams."

"Thanks."

Clint took Davey's hand and entered. Duke Farrell, all five-feet-six of him, came rushing around from behind his desk, his hand extended.

"Clint! By God, you look good."

"Duke."

The two men shook hands.

"And this is the little fella?" Duke asked, looking at the boy.

"This is Davey Wilson," Clint said.

"Hello, Davey."

"Hi, Mr. Duke."

"Come on, both of you. Sit."

Clint and Davey each sat, and Duke went back around his desk. The office was huge, which tended to make Duke look even smaller than he was, except for one thing—he had a large personality.

"What happened to the old place?" Clint asked.

"You'll recall I owned that with Tracker," Duke said, with a sad shrug. "When he was killed, I sold it and started over again."

Abel Tracker was a friend of Clint's, but was much closer with Duke. Clint still felt guilt over the fact that Tracker had been killed while helping him with a job.

"I have a room for you," Duke said.

"That's okay, we're at the Billingham."

"The Billingham?" Duke looked as if he approved. "That's a nice place."

"It sure is," Davey said. "Aunt Laura gave us a room for free."

Duke looked at Clint.

"Aunt Laura?"

"We met the new owner, Laura Dickinson, on the train. She offered us a room."

"You didn't waste much time."

"She likes Davey."

"Ah."

"Where's my Uncle Billy, Mr. Duke?" Davey asked.

"Ah, yes, your Uncle Billy," Duke said. "I can take you to him."

"When?" Clint asked.

"Now, if you like."

"Is it far?"

"Not far, at all," Duke said, standing. "Come with me."

They all stood and left the office. Duke led them down a corridor until they reached the casino. It was twice the size of Duke's old place.

"Impressive operation," Clint said.

"Yes, it is," Duke said. "Uncle Billy is this way."

Chapter Thirty-Three

Duke led Clint and Davey across the room that was crowded with tables and gamblers. Davey stared, his mouth open.

"He's there," Duke said, indicating a table where five men were playing poker.

"It's early," Clint said. "How long has he been playing?"

"Two days," Duke said.

"Does he know we're coming?"

"Yes," Duke said, "I told him. He's prepared to leave the game when you get here."

"After two days?"

"He's well ahead." Duke looked at Clint. "Here or in my office?"

"Your office," Clint said. "I want to get Davey out of here."

"I'll take you back," Duke said, "then I'll come and get him."

Duke accompanied them back to his office, then left to go and fetch Billy Wilson.

"Is my Uncle Billy comin'?" Davey asked.

"He'll be here, Davey," Clint said. "In a minute."

"He's a good poker player, ain't he?"

"Seems like it."

"I wonder if I can beat 'im?"

"You might find out," Clint said, "Let's sit and wait."

"Do you think he'll want me, Clint?" Davey asked, climbing into his chair.

"He'd be a fool not to, Davey," Clint said. "You're a great little boy."

"If he doesn't want me, will you?"

"Well . . . I . . . don't live the kind of life that would be good for a little boy," Clint said. "But you know your Aunt Maddy would want you."

Davey nodded and fell silent, waiting. Several minutes later the door opened, and Duke Farrell entered leading another man.

"Uncle Billy!" Davey cried, springing from the chair and running at the man.

Clint was surprised but pleased that Billy Wilson gathered the boy into his arms and hugged him tightly.

"Davey boy!" he said. "You remember me."

"I remember you," Davey said. "You're funny."

"Wilson," Duke said, "this is Clint Adams. He brought the boy here."

"Saved his life, the way I hear it," Billy Wilson said. He put the boy down and extended his hand. "Mighty appreciative of you bringin' him here to me, Mr. Adams."

"Clint's my friend, Uncle Billy," Davey said.

"I'm sure he is," Wilson said.

William Wilson looked to be in his forties, a little older than Davey's parents had been.

"I'm just glad Davey has some family," Clint said.

Wilson didn't mention his brother or sister-in-law, which Clint assumed was deliberate.

They all sat, Wilson with his nephew on his knee. There was no doubt from the happy look on Davey's face that he recognized his uncle.

"Where are you and Davey stayin'?" Wilson asked.

"The Billingham Hotel," Clint said.

"Nice place," Wilson said. "Right now my room ain't fit for a little boy. I'll need some time to relocate, if you wouldn't mind keepin' him a little longer."

"That's not a problem," Clint said.

"Fine, fine," Wilson said. "Shouldn't take me more than a few days to find a place."

Since he knew his nephew was on arriving, Clint wondered why the man hadn't already found a new place, but he didn't mention it.

"Davey and I still have some unfinished business," Clint said.

Wilson looked puzzled until Davey yelled out, "The zoo!"

Chapter Thirty-Four

Jimbo, Coyote and Henderson got off the train that morning and collected their horses from the stock car.

"Now what?" Henderson asked. "How do we find Adams in this city?"

"First we find a place for ourselves," Jimbo said. "And in a city like San Francisco, it's gonna be hard for the Gunsmith to go unnoticed. He'll be recognized, somethin' will happen, and we'll find 'im."

Coyote said, "Perhaps someone else will kill him."

"Then we'll have to find the boy," Henderson said.

"One thing at a time," Jimbo said. "Let's get a hotel, and a meal."

The train the three men had caught departed hours after Clint's train but skipped many of the stops that train had made. And there hadn't been any trouble, like an explosion in the engine, or a need for water. So it had arrived barely eight hours after Clint and Davey's.

Of course, the three men did not know they were only eight hours behind. But it didn't matter to Jimbo how close or behind they were. He felt sure the Gunsmith's reputation would cause the man to be recognized. If someone didn't try to kill him, someone else would write about his arrival. After all, the Gunsmith was news.

It was just a matter of time.

***

Billy Wilson promised to get in touch as soon as he had a new place to live that he could share with Davey. Uncle and nephew hugged again, and then Wilson left.

"That was my Uncle Billy!" Davey said.

"It sure was," Clint said.

"Now the zoo?" Davey said.

"Now we'll go and pick up Laura," Clint said, "and we'll all go to the zoo."

He and Davey stood.

"I don't know if Wilson will contact you or me when he relocates," Duke said, "but if I hear from him, I'll let you know."

"Same here," Clint said, "and I appreciate all your help, Duke."

"Sure thing," Duke said. "Stop by and try out the new place, Clint."

"Once Davey's settled," Clint said, "I will."

He and Davey left DUKE'S.

When they got back to The Billingham, the clerk told them Laura was in her office and took them to it. Laura was seated behind a modest looking desk and smiled as they entered.

"Uncle Billy?" she said.

"We saw him," Clint said. "He's going to take Billy as soon as he finds a new place to live that would be suitable."

"That's wonderful!" she said, looking at Davey. "Were you excited?"

"Oh boy!" Davey chirped. "Now we go to the zoo."

She smiled.

"Now we go to the zoo."

***

Clint had been to a zoo once, in Philadelphia, when America's first zoo opened in 1874. As it happened, there was no zoo in San Francisco, but something called a "menagerie." It was not large, but big enough to fascinate Davey. After walking through the menagerie, the three of them stopped at a small restaurant for a late lunch.

"So what was Uncle Billy like?" Laura asked, as they ate.

"He's fun!" Davey said.

"He's a gambler," Clint said, "but he left a two-day-long poker game to see Davey."

"Yes, but did he go back to his game afterward?" she asked.

"That I don't know," Clint said. "He said he was going to start looking for a new place."

"He knew Davey was coming," she said. "Why didn't he already have a new place?"

"I wondered the same thing," Clint admitted.

After lunch they returned to the Billingham, where a man was waiting in the lobby for Clint.

"He came in soon after you left, Sir," the clerk said, indicating the man seated on a divan in the lobby.

Clint looked over at the well-dressed man.

"Do you want me to take Davey to my office?" Laura asked. "Or do you still not trust me?"

Laura took Davey by the hand as Clint walked over to the man.

"You looking for me?" he asked.

The man sprang to his feet.

"Mr. Adams?"

"That's right."

"The Gunsmith, right?"

"What do you want?" Clint asked.

"My name is Kerwin," the man said. "I'm with The San Francisco Chronicle."

"And?"

"Well, someone at the train station recognized you, Sir, as you got off the train. I was wondering what brings the Gunsmith to San Francisco? Would you be available for an interview?"

"No interviews," Clint said, "and why I'm here is my business. Now, if you'll excuse me—"

The man reached and grabbed Clint's left arm, then pulled his hand back, as if he had burned it.

"I'm sorry," he said, quickly. "I didn't mean—"

"Mr. Kerwin," Clint said, "we're done. And I better not see my name in your newspaper."

He strode away from the man without looking back.

***

Jimbo, Coyote and Henderson got rooms in a flop-house close to the train depot. Over lunch Jimbo came up with an idea.

"I want you two to go back to the depot and ask around. See if anyone recognized Adams when he got off the train."

"What if he d-d-didn't get off the t-t-train?" Henderson asked.

"Whataya mean? It's the last stop," Jimbo said.

"What if Adams and the k-k-kid got off before the t-t-train got here."

"Where else would they get off?" Jimbo asked.

"Well," Henderson said, "there was a S-S_Sacramento s-s-stop. That's also a big city."

"The word we got in Kellog was that he was goin' to San Francisco," Jimbo said. "That's why we're here."

"And if he is not?" Coyote asked.

Jimbo put his fork down and glared at the two men.

"If he ain't here, then that kid may be talkin' to some lawman, describin' us."

"Then we should head for M-M-Mexico," Henderson said.

"I hate Mexico!" Jimbo said. "Go to the depot and ask around. Let's see what happens before we go off half-cocked and head for Mexico or Sacramento."

"We will go," Coyote said.

"Finish your damn lunch!" Jimbo said, picking up his fork. "We don't know nothin', yet!"

**

After lunch Coyote and Henderson left the flophouse and headed for the train depot.

"Whataya think?" Henderson asked.

"I think we should go to the depot and ask questions."

"Adams may not even be here," Henderson said. "Him and the kid could be anywhere."

"You tell Jimbo that," Coyote suggested.

Chapter Thirty-Five

Clint was at a loss as to what to do with Davey the rest of the day. Laura had a business to run, so he took the boy back to their room and played some poker. He was starting to wonder about dinner when there was a knock at the door. He opened it a crack, saw Laura standing there, and swung it open all the way.

"I don't think you're going to be happy about this," she said, handing him a newspaper. "The evening edition of the Chronicle."

He accepted the paper, backed up to allow her to enter, then read it. It wasn't a headline, but it was prominent. THE GUNSMITH COMES TO TOWN!

"Damn it," Clint said. "I told him . . ."

"What are you going to do?" she asked.

"What can I?" Clint asked. "The damage is done."

"This doesn't necessarily mean that someone will come after you, does it?"

"Not necessarily," he said, "but if the killers followed us here, they'll read it."

"And it says where you're staying," she said. "Will you have to move?"

"Probably."

"But how would they know you came here?"

"If they tracked us to Amarillo, they know," Clint said.

"Then I have a suggestion," she said

"What?"

"Leave Davey with me," she said, "just in case the killers do find you. I can watch him until his uncle is ready to take him."

Clint hesitated.

"You can trust me, Clint," she said. "Believe me."

Clint couldn't see any reason why he shouldn't trust her. So far, she hadn't given any indication to the contrary.

"He'll be safe here," she continued, "I guarantee it."

"All right," he said. "Meanwhile, I'll make sure there are no more write-ups in the Chronicle."

"Are you going to go and see that writer in the morning?"

"Better than that," Clint said. "His boss."

***

The next morning Clint went to the offices of *The San Francisco Chronicle* and asked to see the Editor. The man at the front desk made a phone call, and then another, younger man appeared.

"Mr. Adams? Would you follow me? Mr. Babcock says he'll see you."

Clint followed the young man along several corridors before they came to a door that said EDITOR-AND-CHIEF on it.

"Mr. Adams is here, sir," the young man said.

"Good," the white-haired man behind the desk said. "Now get out!"

"Yessir!"

"And close the door!" the editor shouted.

The young man slammed it firmly.

"Mr. Adams? Have a seat."

Clint sat across from the man.

"What can I do for you?"

"I saw your man Kerwin at my hotel yesterday."

"He told me."

"Did he tell you I said no interviews, and I didn't want my name in your paper?"

"He told me," Babcock said, "but we print news, Mr. Adams. The fact that the Gunsmith is in town is news."

"And you printed it," Clint said. "But I don't want to see my name in your paper again."

"I suppose that's fair," Babcock said, "unless, of course, you decide to shoot someone. That would be news."

"That's not going to happen."

155

"Then if you're not here to shoot anybody," Babcock said, "why *are* you here?"

"As I told your Mr. Kerwin," Clint answered, "that's my business."

"I see," Babcock said. "Well, then I guess we have nothing else to discuss."

Clint stood.

"Keep Kerwin away from me," he said, and left before the editor could say another word.

***

Henderson and Coyote found Jimbo the next morning at a saloon near their flophouse. He was sitting alone, nursing a beer. Several of the tables around him were occupied, but no one was paying any attention to him.

"He was seen at the d-d-depot," Henderson said. "Got off the t-t-train the night before."

"No kiddin'," Jimbo said, slapping his hand down on the newspaper in front of him. "It's in the paper. It also says he's staying at a place called The Billingham."

Coyote and Henderson sat.

"So now what?" Coyote asked.

"We k-k-kill 'im," Henderson said.

"First," we make sure he's got the kid with 'im," Jimbo said, picking up his beer. "Then we kill 'em both."

156

Chapter Thirty-Six

Clint came out of the Chronicle building and hesitated, looking all around him, including the windows and rooftops across the street. Now that his name had appeared in the newspaper, he was going to have to be extra careful. Not only did he have to look out for the killers of Davey's parents, but anyone else who wanted to make a try for the Gunsmith.

If he was going to trust Laura Dickinson with Davey, then he thought he might as well take Duke up on his offer of a room.

He went down the stairs and waved down a horse drawn cab.

"Duke's in Portsmouth Square," he told the driver.

"Yes, Sir."

He climbed aboard and sat back, keeping a sharp eye on the street. When they got to Duke's, he paid the driver and went inside.

The desk clerk recognized him and allowed him to go to Duke's office.

"Didn't expect to see you back here so soon," Duke said, "but I guess you saw the newspaper."

"I saw it," Clint said, seating himself. "I just came from their office."

"Ah, you saw Babcock, then. He's a tough old bird."

"He is that," Clint said.

"Is he gonna keep your name out of the paper the rest of the time you're here?"

"Unless I shoot somebody," Clint said. "Meanwhile, I can't keep Davey with me anymore, so I'll need a room."

"You got one," Duke assured him. "You leavin' the kid with Miss Dickinson?"

"I am," Clint said. "I've decided I can trust her with him. I'll collect my gear and my horse and bring them all over here."

"I've got a livery out back," Duke said.

Clint stood.

"Hopefully, it won't take Bill Wilson long to find himself a new home."

"Once you give the kid to him, there's not much chance those killers will find 'im."

"They probably don't even know there is an uncle," Clint said, "unless they heard that in Kellog when they found out I was coming to San Francisco."

"Somebody there had a big mouth," Duke said.

"Yeah," Clint said, thinking it could only have been the hostler at the livery.

"I should be back in half an hour or so."

"I'll walk you out and get you a key, this way you can go straight to your room."

They walked together to the front desk.

***

Jimbo chose to let Coyote go alone to the Billingham to find Clint. He may have been a half breed, but he knew how to go unseen.

Coyote had found himself a deep doorway to stand in, from where he could see the front door of the Billingham Hotel. He was standing there when Clint's cab stopped in front and let him out. There was no sign of the boy as Clint went into the hotel.

Coyote decided to stay where he was and see what happened next. When Clint came back out, the half breed saw that he was carrying his saddlebags and rifle. He followed Clint at a safe distance and saw him collect his horse from the livery. One horse. Where was the boy?

Clint mounted his horse and rode off, but at a canter. Coyote was able to follow Clint through busy San Francisco streets on foot. Portsmouth Square was even busier, it was easy to follow Clint right to Duke's. A man took Clint's horse from him, and Clint went inside with his saddlebags.

It seemed an obvious conclusion that after the newspaper story had appeared, giving Clint Adams' location, he had chosen to switch hotels. But the question still remained . . . where was the boy?

***

"If he's already put that boy into the law's hands, we might've already had it," Henderson said, when Coyote returned with the news.

"Maybe not," Jimbo said. "We still don't know if the kid can identify us."

"So we wasted all this time," Coyote said. "Came to San Francisco for nothing."

"Maybe," Jimbo said, "but there's still somethin' else we can do."

"What's that?" Henderson asked.

"We can ask the Gunsmith," Jimbo said.

Henderson and Coyote stared at him, and then Henderson said, "You mean . . ."

"I mean grab Adams and make him tell us what the boy knows," Jimbo explained.

"So we gotta face the Gunsmith?" Henderson asked.

"We don't hafta face him," Jimbo said, "we just gotta grab 'im."

Chapter Thirty-Seven

Clint got settled in his room at Duke's, thanked his friend again before leaving for the Billingham, again.

"Anything from Wilson?" he asked, before departing.

"Not a word, yet."

"Is he back in that game?"

"He was," Duke said, "but the game broke up. He's not in the building, anymore."

"So hopefully he's out looking for a place for him and Davey to live," Clint said.

"Let's hope so."

"What do you know about him, Duke?"

"Just that he's a gambler."

"And gamblers aren't known for time spent with children," Clint pointed out.

"You don't think he's sincere?" Duke asked.

"I think maybe he was when he said it," Clint said. "Let's hope he still is."

Clint left and went back to the Billingham to check on Laura and Davey . . .

***

Clint was a bit ashamed of the relief he felt when he found Laura and Davey in Laura's office.

"You look so relieved," Laura said. "Did you think I'd run off with him?"

"Of course not," Clint said.

"Play solitaire for a while, sweetie," Laura said. "I want to talk with Clint."

"Okay."

She and Clint walked to one side and kept their voices low.

"Are you set at Duke's?" she asked,

"Yes, all settled."

"Any word from Davey's Uncle Billy?"

"Not yet," Clint said, "but he's not at Duke's gambling."

"That doesn't mean he's not in some other casino," she pointed out.

"No, it doesn't."

"What will you do if you don't hear from him again?" she asked.

"Are you thinking that, too?" Clint asked.

"The thought had crossed my mind," she said. "He might have been happy to see the boy, and then had second thoughts about accepting the responsibility of raising him."

"Well, I don't know what I'll do," Clint said. "I guess I'll have to cross that bridge if and when I come to it."

Laura looked over at Davey.

"He's a wonderful boy," she said.

"Yes, he is."

Now she looked at Clint.

"Would you keep him?"

"Me?" He looked shocked. "No, not me. I don't lead the kind of life that would be fitting for a small boy."

"You're wonderful with him," she said. "I noticed it immediately on the train."

"He deserves a better life than I could ever give him," he said. "There's a woman in Kellog who'd love to have him."

"His Aunt Maddy."

"Yes," Clint said. "She'd be wonderful for him. And so would you."

"Me?" It was her turn to be shocked. "He doesn't even know me."

"He knows you well enough," Clint said. "But let's put this discussion aside and go to dinner."

"Downstairs?"

"Yes," he said. "I want to stay inside with him until this is all over."

"Very well," she said. "I've already picked out a regular owner's table for myself. Complete with a regular waiter."

"Now," he said, "that's my kind of life."

Chapter Thirty-Eight

They ate their dinner in the hotel dining room, served by a waiter named Arthur, who would be Laura's regular waiter when she dined there.

"There'll be mornings or evenings when I'll dine in my room," she told Clint. "Arthur will be my waiter then, too."

"You never told me what you did back East," he said. "Did you own a hotel there?"

"I didn't," she said. "But I don't want to think about my life back East. It always brings my son to mind, and that's too painful."

"Clint?" Davey said.

"Yes?"

"If you're not stayin' here anymore, will I be in our room alone?"

"No, dear," Laura said. "You're going to stay in my room, now."

"But in our room, I have my own bed."

"And you'll have your own bed in mine, too," she told him.

"You can't stay in our room alone, Davey," Clint said. "It's better if you stay in Laura's."

"Oh, all right," Davey said.

"It'll be fine, Davey," Clint assured him. "Just a few days until your uncle comes to get you," Clint assured him.

"If I go and live with Uncle Billy, will you come, too, Clint?" the boy asked.

"No, Davey," Clint said. "Uncle Billy is your family. I have my own life to live."

"Will you go and see your family?"

"I don't have any family, Davey."

"There's just you?" Davey asked. "That's sad. You could be in my family."

"I don't think your Uncle Billy would like that," Clint said. "Let's just see what happens."

"Oh, okay."

They finished eating and went out to the lobby.

"Will you come up?" Laura asked.

"No, I think I'll go back to Duke's," He lowered his voice. "If anybody finds me or recognizes me and makes a try, I don't want Davey there."

"All right."

" 'night, Davey," Clint said. "I'll see you in the morning."

" 'night, Clint."

"Yes, good-night, Clint," Laura said.

He watched them walk to the stairs and go up, then turned and left the hotel.

***

He stepped from the cab in front of Duke's, looked around carefully before walking to the front door. He stopped there, turned and looked across the street.

They were there. He could feel them.

He went inside.

***

"He sees us!" Henderson said, ducking down.

"No, he doesn't," Jimbo said. "But he feels us."

"He didn't feel me today," Coyote said.

"Maybe not," Jimbo said, "but there's three of us now."

"If he does not see us, perhaps he smells Henderson."

"Hey!"

"Relax," Jimbo said. "The half breed is just proving he has a sense of humor."

"So whatta we do?" Henderson said.

"We pick our time and our spot," Jimbo said. "We'll get 'im, don't worry. Now that we know where he is. Come on. Now's not the time."

Henderson and Coyote started to move.

"Not you," Jimbo said to Coyote.

"Why not?"

"Like you said," Jimbo said, "he won't see or feel you . . .or smell you."

Henderson laughed and said to Coyote, "Now who's laughin'?"

Chapter Thirty-Nine

After breakfast Duke went to work in his office. Clint went to the front window of the lobby and looked across the street. He didn't see anyone, but he still felt someone.

He decided the only way to handle the situation was to put himself out there.

He left the window and went out the door. Walking down the street, he waited for an attack. When it didn't come, he knew why. They still needed to find Davey. They wouldn't try to shoot him from across the street. They would wait until they could grab him.

But there was still somebody on his tail. He was sure of it. That meant he couldn't go anywhere near the Billingham Hotel.

***

Coyote stepped from his doorway and proceeded to follow Clint on foot. He was sure Clint hadn't seen him but was just as sure he felt him. The man had not become a legend without following his instincts.

He continued following at a safe distance, but soon realized what the Gunsmith was doing. He wanted to be attacked, and Coyote certainly wasn't going to do it by himself. He decided that since they had located the Gunsmith and the man wasn't running, he should go back to Jimbo with a suggestion.

Grab Adams now.

***

Clint suddenly felt that the presence behind him was gone. He turned to have a look and saw no one. Could it be they had located Davey and were simply going after him? He changed his plans of wondering and waiting, and headed for the Billingham.

***

"What brings you back here?" Laura asked, when he entered her office.

"I'm not sure," he said. "I suddenly got the feeling this was where I should be."

"Are you expecting those men to come here?"

"I wasn't'," Clint said. "I was sure they were watching me, but then the feeling was gone."

"I can have my dealers watch out for trouble," Laura said.

"No," Clint said, "I don't want any innocents to get hurt."

"So you'll face these men on your own?"

"That's the way they want it," Clint said, "and so do I."

"Clint?"

Clint looked down as Davey tugged at his arm.

"Yeah, Davey?"

"Are you gonna kill the men who killed my ma and pa?" the boy asked.

Clint studied the boy for a moment, before answering.

"We're going to have to see what happens, Davey."

The boy stared straight ahead and said, "I wanna kill them." His eyes filled with tears, and Clint felt he was finally going to give in to his grief.

"Davey—" Laura started, but Clint held up his hand to stop her.

"I won't let you do that, Davey," Clint said. "You're too young to kill anyone."

"Then you'll have to kill them for me."

"Like I said," Clint replied, "let's see what happens." He looked at Laura. "Keep him here. I'm going to have a look outside."

"All right."

Clint left the office and walked back to the lobby.

***

"Face the Gunsmith?" Henderson asked Coyote. "Is that what you're suggesting?"

Coyote spoke to Jimbo, not Henderson.

"He wants to play games with us," the half breed said. "He thinks he can lead us around by the nose. I believe we should show him he cannot."

Jimbo thought a moment, then said, "This sounds good."

"Ya wanna know what I think?" Henderson asked.

"No!" Jimbo said. He looked at the half breed. "Do you have a plan?"

"I do."

"Then let's hear it . . ."

***

Clint went to the front door of the Billingham and stared out. He could see or feel no one. Apparently, they weren't going to play by his rules. He was going to have to play by theirs.

He went back to Laura's office.

"I want you to stay in here, no matter what you hear," he told her. "And keep Davey here."

"All right, Clint," she said, "but be careful."

"I'm always careful."
He left the office, again.

***

In the end, he decided not to play exactly by their rules but to add a little something of his own. He decided to pull a chair up in front of the hotel, just to the left of the front door, sit and wait.

***

"Which hotel?" Henderson asked. "The Billingham or Duke's?"
Jimbo looked at Coyote, who had slowly moved into the position of calling the play.
"When he went into Duke's, the boy wasn't with him," the half breed said. "I think the boy is in the Billingham."
"Who would Adams trust enough to watch the boy?" Jimbo asked.
"I suppose we'll have to find that out," Coyote said.
"Right," Jimbo said. "The Billingham."

***

They approached the hotel carefully, and from down the street they could see Clint sitting on the porch.

"What's he tryin' to pull n-n-now?" Henderson asked.

"He's tryin' to let us know he ain't worried," Jimbo said. "He looks relaxed."

"He is not," Coyote said. "He is alert."

"You know," Jimbo said, "we don't have to go in the front door."

"W-w-whatta we gonna do, check every r-r-room?" Henderson asked.

"No," Jimbo said, "we're gonna ask questions. If any-body knows where that kid is, it'd be the desk clerk."

"So whatta we d-d-do?"

"You stay here and watch," Jimbo said. "Me and Coyote will find another way in."

"And w-w-what do I do if he gets up and goes in-side?" Henderson asked.

"Then you move your ass and go in after him," Jimbo said. "It's gonna be up to you to warn us."

Chapter Forty

Clint could feel eyes on him. His instincts were that good. They must have arrived on the train right after his. They were waiting for him to lead them to Davey, but how long would they be content to just watch him? At some point somebody was going to have to make a move, and he would be ready.

***

Jimbo and Coyote found their way to the rear of the hotel, where they found a door. It was a decent door made of good wood, with a good lock, but Coyote was able to open it. They slipped inside, where it was dark.

"Looks like a storeroom," Jimbo said.

They saw a closed door across the room with light streaming in from around and underneath. Jimbo indicated the door and Coyote led the way.

They found it unlocked, and when they opened it saw a long corridor.

"Let's see if we can get to the lobby," Jimbo said, keeping his voice low.

Coyote nodded and led the way down the corridor.

They came to a fork. If they went left it looked like a back staircase to the second floor. Right seemed likely to lead to the lobby.

They moved along that corridor until they saw an opening up ahead. When they reached it, they saw that it led right out to the lobby. From their vantage point they could see the front desk and the front door. For a brief moment Jimbo considered coming at the Gunsmith from the door, but then decided against it. They needed to find that boy, first.

The desk clerk looked like a young man who was likely to scare when presented with a gun barrel. Jimbo nudged Coyote to move forward.

They came out of the corridor into the lobby and moved to the front desk. By the time the clerk became aware of them, they were on him.

"Just relax," Jimbo said, pointing his gun at the man.

"Huh? Wha—"

"We've got some questions for you," Jimbo said. "If you answer, you'll be fine. If you don't, my half breed friend here will probably want to cut out your tongue. I don't know if I'd be able to stop him."

"H-half breed?" the clerk stammered.

"Half Apache," Jimbo said.

"Apache!" The clerk's eyes were wide with fright, which was what Jimbo wanted.

"Do you understand?" Jimbo asked.

"Y-Yessir."

"Clint Adams is a guest here, isn't he?"

"Uh, yessir," the clerk said. "I mean, no Sir."

"Which is it?"

"He *was* a guest here, but he checked out."

"He's sittin' on the front porch," Jimbo said.

"Yessir, but he no longer has a room."

"All right," Jimbo said, "but when he checked in, he had a little kid with 'im."

"Oh, uh, yessir," the clerk said, keeping his eye on Coyote, who looked like a savage to him.

"Where's the boy?"

"With Miss Dickinson."

"Who's that?"

"Laura Dickinson," the clerk said. "She's the new owner."

"And where is she?"

"In her office."

"Where's that?"

"In the back."

"You're gonna take us there."

"Uh . . ."

"Or I'll turn you over to my friend."

The clerk stared at Coyote, his eyes beginning to water.

"Let's go," Jimbo said.

***

Henderson was getting impatient and spooked at the prospect of facing the Gunsmith alone. All he could think to do was get closer to the hotel, so he could get a decent shot.

He broke from the cover of his doorway and moved toward the hotel.

***

Clint didn't know why, but he leaned over in his chair to have a look at the lobby. He saw that the front desk was unmanned. He didn't immediately think it meant anything. But the longer the clerk was away, the less he liked it. Finally, he decided to go into the lobby and check. As he stood up, he heard something behind him . . .

***

All Henderson could think to do when Adams stood up and started into the hotel was shoot the man in the back. It seemed his only option.

He drew his gun . . .

Chapter Forty-One

When the clerk opened the office door, Laura looked up from her desktop, which was covered with cards. Davey was sitting with his back to the door but was concentrating on the cards in his hand.

"What is it—" she started to ask the clerk, but then she saw the man behind him, and the guns. She started to get up.

"Stay sittin', lady," Jimbo said. He pushed the clerk. "You get over there."

The clerk hurriedly moved to one side.

At this point, Davey turned to look.

"Who're you?" he asked.

"This's gotta be the kid," Jimbo said.

"What kid is that?" Laura asked.

"The one we're lookin' for," he said. "The one who might be able to identify us."

"I'm sorry," she said, "but this is my son, Harry. I don't know what you're talking about."

Jimbo looked at the clerk.

"Is this the kid Clint Adams came in with?"

The clerk looked at Laura, but when Coyote moved toward him, he jerked his eyes away from her.

"Y-yes, it is," he said.

"That's it," Coyote said, and pointed his gun at Davey.

"Not here!" Jimbo said. "Somebody'll hear the shot."

"I can fix that," Coyote said. He put his gun away and drew his knife.

"We hafta kill all three of them," Jimbo said. He pointed his gun toward the clerk and said, "Start with him."

Coyote advanced on the clerk, but then they heard the shots.

***

Clint saw a man with his gun already in his hand, obviously intending to shoot him in the back. That was something Clint Adams would never allow.

He drew and fired. The bullet struck the man in the chest, bringing a surprised look to his face. He fired a shot into the ground, and then dropped his gun and toppled to the ground after it. Clint walked to the body to check that he was dead, then realized why the clerk wasn't in the lobby.

The back door.

"Damn!" he swore and ran into the hotel as a crowd gathered.

Clint headed directly to Laura's office. As he slammed the door open the room seemed empty, until he looked to the left. The clerk was on the ground in a bloody heap. He went to the young man and saw that he had been gutted with a knife. Laura and Davey had either been taken, or they hadn't been in the office. They could still be in Laura's room.

He ran to the second floor to check. After forcing the door, he found her room empty, as well.

He ran back down to the lobby, and stopped short when he saw two uniformed policeman pointing guns at him.

"Stop right there!" one shouted.

"You don't understand," Clint said, holding out his empty hands.

"What's to understand?" one of them asked. "Did you shoot that man out front?"

"Well, yes, but he was trying to shoot me in the back."

A third policeman came out of the corridor that led to Laura's office.

"We got another one back here, gutted.

"Mister," one said, "just drop the gun and keep your hands up."

"My name is Clint Adams," Clint said, obeying. "Miss Dickinson and a little boy are in danger."

181

"Who's Dickinson?" one of them asked.

"The new owner of this hotel," Clint said. "Look, she's in trouble and she has a little boy with her."

"You said the man outside was trying to shoot you in the back," one said.

"That's right."

"What did the man in the office do?" he asked. "Why'd you stab him?"

"I didn't stab him," Clint said. "I don't even have a knife."

The three policemen exchanged glances with each other.

"Look," Clint asked, "who's in charge?"

"Our boss will be here soon," one of them said. "So we'll just wait."

"The longer we wait the more trouble Miss Dickinson and the boy are in," Clint argued.

"Mister," one policeman said, "you're in a lot of trouble yourself."

The older of the three policemen suddenly said to Clint, "What did you say your name was?"

"Clint Adams."

It was obvious he recognized the name.

"Jesus," the officer said.

Chapter Forty-Two

Clint considered making a break for the door, but the three officers, having realized who he was, kept a sharp eye—and their guns—trained on him. So he sat in the lobby and waited. Eventually a man dressed in a three-piece suit entered the lobby and spoke to the police officers. When he approached Clint, they kept their guns on him.

"Mr. Adams?" the man said. "I'm Lieutenant Colby."

Clint had been to San Francisco many times, had occasionally had to deal with the police, but found that personnel there changed very often. He had never found the same man there twice. This was no exception. He had never seen Colby before.

The Lieutenant was middle-aged, neatly dressed and clipped.

"Lieutenant," he said, "a woman and small boy are in deadly danger, and the longer you keep me here, the worse it gets."

"If that's true, we'll be glad to help you find them," Colby said, "but you must understand we have to determine what the truth is."

"Normally I'd be right with you, but there isn't time. Do you know Duke Farrell?"

"Mr. Farrell is well known in San Francisco," Colby said, "and respected."

"He'll vouch for me," Clint said. "And support my story. Get him here."

Colby thought a moment, then said, "That's a good way to go. We'll get him here as soon as possible."

Colby turned and spoke to the police officers again. One of them holstered his gun and ran from the lobby.

***

"As soon as possible," turned out to be a half-an-hour, during which Clint became more and more agitated.

Lt. Colby used the time to get Clint's story, which he would check with Duke Farrell when the hotel/casino owner arrived.

Finally, Duke walked into the lobby and Colby went to confer with him. Then both men walked to Clint and Lt. Colby told his men, "Put up your guns."

Clint stood as Colby said, "Mr. Farrell corroborates your story, Mr. Adams. We'll do what we can to help."

"Clint, I'm so sorry," Duke said. "The Lieutenant will help and so will I. I have men I can put on this."

"We need to find out if anyone saw them leaving this hotel," Clint said. "Or if anyone saw two men with a woman and a child anywhere in the city. I'm just hoping they're still alive."

"Give us a description of the woman and the boy and I'll send it out," Colby said.

After he had written the descriptions down the Lieutenant left the lobby with his men.

"Don't be too hard on Colby," Farrell said. "He was just doin' his job."

"I know that," Clint said, "this just wasn't the time for me to run into a man willing to do his job."

"Let's get back to my place and I'll put my men on this. Colby'll keep some men here."

Duke had a carriage waiting outside. It was a short ride to his place in Portsmouth Square.

In the lobby Clint asked, "Any word from Uncle Billy?"

"No," Duke said, "I haven't heard from him or seen him."

They got to Duke's office and Clint said, "I'm not going to be able to just sit and wait."

"As soon as we get a sniff we'll have someplace to go," Duke said. "Let me get my boys on it. Meanwhile, have a drink and try to calm down."

Duke left the office and Clint poured himself a whiskey from a decanter Duke had on a sideboard. He sat down and sipped his drink. He wanted to get up and get moving, but there was no place to go.

Eventually, while working on a second drink, Duke entered the office and sat at his desk.

"I've got men on it, and the San Francisco police are on it," he said. "They won't be able to get on a train or a boat to leave the city."

"They might kill Laura and the boy and just ride out," Clint said.

"I'm checking hotels outside of Portsmouth Square," Duke said. "That seems most likely."

"Don't forget there were three men," Clint said.

"Yes, I put the word out to look for a hotel where three men registered in the last day or so. Also, where two men may now be with a woman and a child."

"There's a lot of places to hide in a city this big," Clint said.

"Yes," Duke said, "if you're from here and know the city well. They don't. They'll be in a hotel, at least until tomorrow, when they try to get out of the city."

"We better find them before then," Clint said.

"If the woman and boy are already dead . . ."

". . . then I want them even more," Clint finished.

Chapter Forty-Three

Clint remained in Duke's office, alternating between sitting and pacing. He felt completely responsible for Laura and Davey being taken from the Billingham. His decision to sit in front of the hotel had to have pushed the men to enter by a back door and make a fool of him while he sat out front and waited. Laura and Davey had to pay the ultimate price for his stupidity. This was a mistake he would never have made a few years ago. He only hoped the men would go after him before Davey.

He had Duke send a telegram to Kellog, Texas to the sheriff there, asking if he had made any progress figuring out who the killers were. So while waiting to hear from "Uncle Billy," waiting for word from Duke's men or the police, he was also waiting for a telegram.

Clint was normally very good at waiting, but that was when he was the one causing the wait.

The first thing to arrive was a telegram from Kellog. The sheriff had made no progress.

"That figures," Clint said, wadding the telegram up and tossing it into a corner. "He probably gave up after I left town."

"You told me the mayor was on his back."

"Maybe he gave up his badge when I left," Clint said. "Doesn't matter. There's no help there."

"So there's nothing to do but just continue waiting . . ." Duke said.

Clint nodded.

They had food brought into the office, but Clint only picked at it. Finally, one of Duke's men came in and spoke to him in a low tone.

"Don't whisper, for Pete's sake," Duke said.

"Sorry. Lieutenant Colby is here."

"Well, bring him in."

Clint stood as the man left and sent Colby in.

"Any progress?" Clint asked.

"Nothing yet," Colby said, "but I thought you'd like to know that no bodies have been found, female or child."

"I suppose that's good," Clint said.

"Nothing from your men, Duke?" Colby asked.

"Not yet."

"Well, they haven't taken a stage or a boat, or a train. They're probably still here."

"If they haven't ridden out."

"With a woman and a boy?" Colby asked. "They'd be noticed. If they're going to try riding out, they'll have to kill the woman and boy, and then get horses. We've got most of the livery stables covered."

"There are private ones, though," Clint said, "and other places to buy horses."

"Yes, there are."

"Well, thanks for filling us in, Lieutenant," Duke said.

"If I get anything else I'll let you know," Colby said. "And if you find out anything . . ."

". . . you'll be the first we tell," Duke said.

Colby nodded and left.

"After I take care of them," Clint said.

"Clint—"

"Don't worry, Duke," Clint said. "I won't get you in trouble with the law. If we hear anything, I'll just need a little head start."

Chapter Forty-Four

Somebody came to Duke's door later that afternoon and knocked. Duke answered and held a short conversation there, then turned to Clint and snapped, "We got 'em!"

"Where?"

"A flophouse near the train depot," Duke said. "Three men checked in, and now they have a woman and a child."

"Exactly where is this place?"

"My man'll show you. He's waitin' outside."

"Stay here, Duke," Clint said. "And give me that head start I mentioned."

"I'll wait a half hour and then notify Colby."

"That'll do it," Clint said. "Thanks."

Duke opened his door, revealing the thirtyish man outside.

"This is Torrence. He'll take you."

"Let's go!" Clint said to Torrence.

***

"Why are we still here?" Coyote asked. "We should have killed them where we found them."

"Adams was too close," Jimbo said. "At the sound of a shot he would've been right on us."

"What about now?" Coyote asked. "We can kill them right here and be gone."

"Where?" Jimbo said. "There's no train, we have no horses—"

"We can get horses," Coyote said.

"By now they're lookin' for us," Jimbo said. "They've got livery stables covered."

"We do not buy horses," Coyote said. "We steal them."

"Four horses?"

"Two!" Coyote snapped. "We kill them and leave them here."

Laura sat on the bed with her arms protectively around Davey. It was still vivid in her mind the way her desk clerk had looked when Coyote stuck his knife in his belly. She hadn't even gotten to the point where she remembered the young man's name.

"If we ride out, Adams will be on our trail."

"We take care of him when we are away from here," Coyote said. "I'm starting to think you are afraid of him."

"Hey," Jimbo said, "I was never the one who said I wanted to face him. That was you."

"I will still face him," Coyote said. "But we must get him away from here so he will not have any help. The law here will not follow us."

"They better not," Jimbo said. "We don't need a whole damned posse after us."

"Posses come from Western towns," Coyote said. "The law here is more Eastern than Western. Once we leave San Francisco, they will forget us." Coyote looked at the woman and child and put his hand on his knife. "Let me have them now."

Jimbo looked at them, as well, then at Coyote.

"Go out and get us two horses first," Jimbo said. "Once we kill them I wanna be gone."

Coyote headed for the door.

"I will return."

***

Torrence had a carriage out front and drove Clint to the hotel, a rundown building with no name anywhere on the front. They stopped down the street and walked to it, staying across the street.

"What room?" Clint asked.

"Seven," Torrence said. "Second floor."

"Stay here," Clint said. "You've done your part."

He started across the street, but Torrence grabbed his arm.

"Wait!" the man said, "That's one of them. He's a half breed."

Clint saw the man coming out the front door. He was sure this half breed was the one whose presence he felt.

"Wanna take 'im?" Torrence asked.

"I want to get the woman and child safe first," Clint said. "Then I'll take them. Let's give him some time to get away, and then I'll go in. You stay here."

"Right," Torrence said. "I'll let you know if he starts back."

"Good."

Clint hurried across the street and into the hotel. The tired looking clerk seemed surprised to see him.

"If I was you," Clint said, "I'd take a walk."

"Whatever you say," the clerk said, and rushed out from behind the desk.

Clint went up the stairs and made his way to room seven. There was no use in pussyfooting, as the floor-boards creaked loudly. He didn't bother knocking, just drew his gun and kicked in the door.

One man was in the room, standing next to Laura and Davey, who were sitting on the bed. He held his gun to Laura's head. Clint wondered why he had chosen her instead of the boy. After all, Davey was the center of all this.

"Clint Adams?" the man asked.

"You have me at a disadvantage," Clint said.

"My name's not important," Jimbo said. "What did you do with the half breed?"

"I let him go," Clint said. "I get the feeling you're the one I want."

"You might want me," Jimbo said, "but I have you, don't I?"

"Maybe not."

Jimbo frowned.

"You're pointing your gun at the lady, but it's the boy I want."

Jimbo took a second to think. In that second, when he was moving the gun barrel from Laura to Davey, Clint fired. The bullet hit him in the shoulder and spun him around, his gun flying across the room.

"Oh God!" Laura shrieked, and hugged Davey, who was stiff in her arms.

Clint moved quickly to check Jimbo, who was lying on his side, clutching his shoulder.

"Coyote will kill you," the man said.

"The half breed?" Clint asked.

"He'll be back."

"I'm counting on it."

"Thank God!" Laura said. "They were going to kill us."

"Not anymore," Clint said.

Footsteps came pounding down the hallway and then Lieutenant Colby appeared, followed by uniformed policemen. He came up short and looked at the man on the floor.

"Is he dead?"

"Not a chance."

Colby turned to his men.

"Pick him up," he said.

They grabbed Jimbo and hauled him onto his feet. As they dragged him out Colby asked Clint, "What's his name?"

"Don't know, and don't care," he answered. "I'm just glad the boy, and Miss Dickinson, are safe."

"And the other man?"

"A half breed," Clint said. "He was leaving as I arrived."

"You let him go?"

"I figured he was getting them transportation," Clint said. "If your men wait here, I think they might get him as a horse thief."

"Oh, they'll get him, all right."

"Make sure you leave enough of them," Clint advised. "I think he's handy with a knife."

"Four should do it," Colby said.

"Probably," Clint said. "I'd like to take Miss Dickinson and the boy back to the Billingham."

"Go ahead," Colby said. "I can get her story later."

Clint looked at Laura and Davey and said, "Let's get out of here."

Laura stood and as they each took one of Davey's hands, Clint noticed the boy was still very stiff.

Chapter Forty-Five

Clint reclined on his back, listening to the sleeping Laura breathe next to him. As he had suspected, when they got back to her hotel, Davey had a full-blown breakdown, screaming and crying for his mom. It was heartbreaking to hear. They called for a doctor, and the boy was now in a hospital, under observation.

Once he was taken care of, Laura fell into Clint's arms. Clint was sure she was seeking solace, but he also knew that their coupling was hanging in the air between them from the beginning.

She was a lovely woman, sleek and smooth, and while she was a lady, the lovemaking was feverish and fierce, probably an effort to feel as alive as she could after her experience.

Clint had heard from Lt. Colby that Coyote had returned with two stolen horses, and had immediately been arrested. He had managed to injure one officer with his knife, but the other three had subdued him. With the man named Jimbo and the half breed, Coyote, in custody, Davey was safe.

Laura stirred, turned her head and looked at him.

"I'm hungry."

"We can have supper."

She reached out a hand and grasped his cock.

"Not hungry for food," she said.

"Ah," he said, turning toward her.

This time was less fierce, more gentle. He tried to give her what she wanted, what she needed, and seemed to be doing the job nicely.

Rather than grasp him and pull him to her, she settled down on her back and allowed him to settle between her thighs, pressing his face to the tangle of hair there, probing with his tongue until he found her wet and ready . . .

***

The next morning, after breakfast, Clint went to the San Francisco Police Department headquarters and asked for Lt. Colby. He was shown to the man's office and sat.

"How's the boy?" Colby asked.

"In the hospital," Clint said. "The doctor wanted to observe him for a while after he broke down. I'll go and see him after this."

"And the lady?"

"Much better, ready to speak with you later today."

"And how are you?" Colby asked. "Satisfied with the outcome?"

"Yes," Clint said, "especially after a telegram this morning from Kellog."

"Good news?"

"The sheriff there found the man who hired those fellas to kill Davey's parents. And they also happened to kill the town doctor."

"Who hired them?"

"A rancher who lived nearby," Clint said. "He wanted their land and Wilson wouldn't sell. Now he's in jail."

"A fitting end for him," Colby said. "Your two are in our jail. I'll be in touch with the law in Kellog and I'm sure we can have them charged with murder, as well as kidnapping and horse thievery."

"So you don't need me?"

"I don't think so," Colby said. "Miss Dickinson's testimony should be enough."

"That's it, then," Clint said. "I'll go and see the boy."

Both men stood.

"What will happen to the boy?"

"His uncle seems to have done a disappearing act," Clint said. "I think he got scared. But there are two very nice ladies who'd be willing to take him. He'd be lucky to end up with either one."

"Hopefully, he'll get to make the choice."

The two men shook hands.

"Thanks for your help, Lieutenant."

Clint left the office, and the building, heading for the hospital.

***

When he entered Davey's room the boy was staring straight ahead. The doctor said he had never seen a child handle shock that way.

"He hasn't cried for his parents?" the doctor had asked Clint when they first met.

"Not til today."

The doctor took Davey into the hospital immediately. Now the child had been there overnight.

"Davey," Clint said.

The boy turned his head and looked at him.

"Hello, Clint."

"How are they treating you?"

"Okay," Davey said, "but I want my Uncle Billy."

"We're still waiting for him to let us know where he is."

"I want him," Davey said. "He's my family."

"I know, Davey." He couldn't bear to tell the boy he thought Billy Wilson had run away from the prospect of raising his nephew.

"Mr. Adams?"

He turned and saw a nurse looking in.

"Yes."

"There's a gentlemen out here who wishes to see you."

"I'll be right there." He looked at Davey. "Be right back."

He stepped into the hall and was surprised to see Billy Wilson.

"Wilson."

The man looked at Clint and shrugged.

"I admit I panicked," Wilson said, "but I'm here now. Mrs. Dickinson told me Davey was here."

"He finally had a full-fledged breakdown, Wilson," Clint said. "He's going to need care."

"I'll take care of him," Wilson said. "He was my brother's son. He's my family. I'll care for him, Mr. Adams."

"And you won't panic again?"

"I won't panic again," the man assured him.

"Well, then," Clint said, "he's in there, asking for you."

"Thanks, Adams, for all you've done."

"I'm finished," Clint said. "The rest of this boy's life is up to you."

Wilson nodded and entered the hospital room. As Clint walked down the hall he heard Davey cry out, "Uncle Billy!"

Upcoming New Release

J.R. ROBERTS
THE GUNSMITH
477
SHERIFF IRON HORSE

Since no one else will take the job as Sheriff of Hellcat, Arizona, eastern educated Apache named Iron Horse takes the job. When he gets in over his head, with no deputies and no one else in town to help him, Clint Adams again find himself in the position of helping a friend stay alive.

For more information
visit: www.SpeakingVolumes.us

  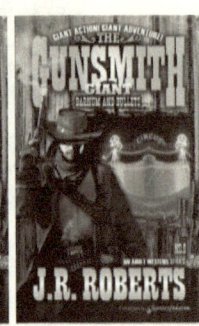

On Sale Now!

Award-Winning Author
Robert J. Randisi (J.R. Roberts)

**For more information
visit: www.SpeakingVolumes.us**